Tiki Vampires

FEVER

A.J. LLEWELLYN and
D.J. MANLY

Fever
ISBN # 978-1-78184-696-4
©Copyright A.J. Llewellyn and D.J. Manly
Cover Art by Posh Gosh ©Copyright 2013
Interior text design by Claire Siemaszkiewicz
Totally Bound Publishing

Published in 2014 by Totally Bound Publishing, Newland House, The Point, Weaver Road, Lincoln, LN6 3QN, United Kingdom.

Praise for

A.J. Llewellyn and D.J. Manly

Hawaiian gods? Vampires? Curses and dire consequences? Sign me on!... 'Tiki Vampires' promises to be an excellent addition to these authors' work and my bookshelves, and if this first book is anything to judge it by, I'll be hanging on by my fingernails — as usual. I cannot wait!
~ *Rainbow Book Reviews*

Totally Bound Publishing books by A.J. Llewellyn and D.J. Manly:

FEVER

Dedication

To Jepoi Jourdain Donovan Genaldo for letting us
have our way with his name! We love you, Jepoi!

Prologue

The idea that things always remain as they were meant to be is a myth. Humans have no idea the games gods play behind the scenes and the havoc it creates in their lives. How very fragile the periods of peace are, those seen and unseen by the human eye.

I know this first-hand because I am Kane, Hawaiian god of the forest and trees. I am worshipped as ancestor of both chiefs and commoners. I give life. I make the sun rise and set. I rule the upper heaven of gods, the lower heavens above the earth, and earth itself where I maintain a garden for all mortals to enjoy.

Unlike my counterpart, Kanaloa, I have nothing to do with the dead, or with evil. And no sacrifice is required to thank me for my gifts.

Since the beginning, I have resided in an uneasy alliance with Kanaloa, god of death and darkness. Like a longtime married couple, we have often been at war with each other. Several times I cast Kanaloa down to the underworld with the spirits he keeps as his slaves. He always returns.

I expect as much.

Kanaloa and I have a relationship which much resembles the elements of nature, the rising and falling of the waves ferociously crashing on the rocks, the sputtering of a volcano, with scalding lava forever threatening to overflow. Be it earth-shattering sex or earthshaking fury, Kanaloa has been a partner in this with me.

Until now.

Something inconceivable has happened and if naught is rectified, I fear for humankind. I shudder to think of the damage Kanaloa can do reigning on his own. Imbalance, jealousy, lust and greed—all familiar to Kanaloa. He has cast upon me a curse I know not how to reverse.

And as I stand on the beach in the world of mortal men watching the waves, I remember…

Kanaloa climbed to me on his hands and knees across the huge round bed. There was a look in his eyes which spoke to me of lust and depravity. He wanted to restrain me, to make me submit to his pleasure, and yet, we were equal in all ways, merely mirror images of one another.

"Except you are by far the more beautiful," Kanaloa whispered.

He'd heard my thoughts. I could keep nothing from him, which infuriated me at times. I glanced overhead. Rings of pure gold extended from the skies and clutched my wrists, and I was hauled up to a standing position on the bed. I struggled, but the rings tightened as Kanaloa's gaze lighted upon them. It was futile to deny him. I could open the rings only to see them close instantly again, which could potentially go on for hours.

On his knees in front of me, he raised his eyes, brown with gold flecks, the contrast to my blue ones. His golden hair hung in waves down his back as was the case with my black hair, less wavy, thicker. I met his gaze, my lips quivering in a smile. "Happy now?"

"Always." Kanaloa heaved a sigh, his hands moving over my naked calves. He stroked me, caressing the taut muscles then moved up to my thighs. "You could make the stars in the sky weep at your beauty, Kane." His tongue darted out and licked the head of my cock. One lick. I was already erect, often in that state. I wasn't quite sure if that was a result of my immortality or just because my thoughts were consumed with erotic possibilities.

"You are, after all, the god of procreation," Kanaloa murmured. He let his tongue make a circle around my cock.

A shiver ran up my spine. I knew he would tease then withhold satisfaction until I broke my bonds and took him by force. He enjoyed this game, and usually I enjoyed playing it except...well... I had something else on my mind...or I should say, someone else on my mind.

Strong hands clasped my ass cheeks. "Spread your legs wider!"

I widened my stance and grunted as Kanaloa buried his face in my groin. He played there for a few minutes, licking and suckling until he swallowed the head of my cock, scraping his teeth on my scrotum. His idea of foreplay always involved pain. He swallowed more of my cock and invaded my ass with several fingers. He found the spot he knew would make me his slave for some time and worked it with his fingers until I ground my teeth together. With his fingers working my super sensitive prostate and my cock down his throat, I was more than his prisoner. I suppose it was the only time I was truly his to do with as he pleased, but then, I could have him equally so, and he knew it.

I cried out softly and he came off my cock, which was still hard, still throbbing. He left his fingers inside my ass, just lightly moving in and out, and smiled up at me. I looked down at him, at his smug look of satisfaction, and scowled. "You can do better I'm sure."

He didn't like that but I never knew Kanaloa to back down from a challenge. It was this pride of his which had helped him escape from Hell where I'd sent him more than once. "Oh I can," he sneered, close to my face. "My beautiful Kane." He grabbed the back of my neck and kissed me, open mouth, tongue mingling with mine. I tasted sweetness, and yet there was that acid aftertaste, reminding me of who he was.

He moved his hands over my muscled chest and toyed with my nipples, pulling and biting as my hips swayed forward in spite of my attempt at defiance. My cock, hard and erect, dripping with need, brushed Kanaloa's belly as he rubbed his thumbs across my nipples, working them into stiff nubs. His tongue flicked across them and I felt several hands smoothing over the back of my legs, heard groans of greed and lust floating up to my ears. "I see you've brought company," I managed, my chest heaving, nipples aching as he took one between his teeth and pulled.

Kanaloa stood back to admire his handiwork, his own cock bloated and dripping. "How your nipples stand out, glistening and hard." His eyes glowed, his gaze moving down to my cock. He held his cock to mine as I felt hands spreading my ass cheeks.

Demon spirits with their long, wet tongues invaded my ass. I grunted, my teeth grinding together as Kanaloa lifted my cock in his hand. He lightly fondled it, leaning forward to lick and nibble my nipples again, then those tongues began to fuck me ever so slowly, in and out, ever expanding, thickening, over and over until I practically begged Kanaloa to give me relief.

I knew he wouldn't. I knew what he wanted. And oh, I was ripe to give it to him. He held my cock in such a way, he knew I couldn't come. "You want it?" I baited him. "You want my cock, Kanaloa?" I pushed forward against his body. I could tell he too couldn't wait much longer. He ran his hands over my ribcage, licked my chest, squeezed my cock and massaged my balls, and suddenly the demons withdrew. I could hear their cries of protest as Kanaloa gave the order.

He was on his knees now, his creamy, white buttocks in the air, teasing me. "If you want to fuck, Kane," he mocked, "show me what you're made of. God of warriors? Ha!" He waved his ass in the air and I broke the restraints.

I lunged for him, and parting that ass I dove into him with my tongue, not yet prepared to give him what he craved. I had some satisfaction knowing that only I, Kane, could give it to him.

"Kane, please!" He turned to look at me with pleading eyes.

I pushed his head into the sheets. "Not yet, when I'm ready." I'd never realised how much I despised his character. I guess I wasn't supposed to. I was just supposed to accept who we were, what we were – I, the good one, balancing his propensity to do harm, and Kanaloa, giving me the job of policing his evil.

But I'd found a more pleasant something to occupy my time with recently, and his name was Delmontre. He was a mortal, a servant to the gods, chosen for his beauty and other attributes. Our love was forbidden and that thrilled me. So, I guess you could say that I had a touch of the bad boy in me as well.

I slapped Kanaloa's ass a few times, revelling in his whimpered pleading then grabbed his hips and torpedoed him big time. I showed no mercy, doing exactly as he craved. Would it temper his behaviour? No. Would he change his ways? No. Because that's the way it was meant to be.

I had no idea that Kanaloa knew of my affair with Delmontre at that time. Nor was I aware of Delmontre's ambition to escape his mundane condition. The earth rumbled as I took Kanaloa and when I'd finished, I pulled away and summoned the servants to bring wine and cheese.

I lay on the huge round bed, covered with sweat and come, and thought of being with Delmontre.

If I'd ever known love, it was with the mortal. What Kanaloa and I had was not love. It was a strange kind of counter-affection that was soaked with rivalry and strife. I thought Delmontre loved me, truly loved me…that was, until he betrayed me.

And Kanaloa eventually took a lot of pleasure in informing me of that betrayal. It still hurt. It hurt so much I couldn't say his name for some time.

When Kanaloa disappeared from my chambers without a word, I thought nothing of it. He was prone to do that. We didn't have much in common except when we were fucking. He did his thing. I did mine.

The servants prepared a bath for me and I was luxuriating in it, staring at the clouds swimming around me when the door flew open. Kanaloa paraded in.

I glanced up, a glass of wine in my hand. I raised it to my lips and regarded him curiously as he floated over to me in a long, white robe.

"What do you want now?" I asked, not unkindly.

"To talk about your indiscretion with that servant." He practically spat on the floor.

I lifted an eyebrow.

"I know, you see." His brown-eyed gaze seemed to bore into mine.

I shrugged. "You intend on making a big deal out of it?"

"I could report you to the council."

"Go ahead." I took a swallow of wine and licked my lips. I knew it was a minor indiscretion. I'd receive a slap on the wrist.

Kanaloa's gaze settled on my mouth for a moment then he uttered a harsh laugh. "It's betrayal."

"Betrayal of whom?"

"You have no right to take a mortal lover, not without me. We share him."

"No," I said.

"You have...feelings for this...mortal boy?"

"He isn't a boy, and my feelings are none of your business. He is mine. So" —I rose from the tub and motioned to a servant for a towel — "keep your distance."

I was not prepared for his rage. With a swoop of his hand, he broke everything in the room then he pointed outward and brought lightning to the sky.

A terrified servant handed me a towel. I wiped my chest and my face and watched Kanaloa from a distance, waiting for more. "Finished?"

He placed his hands on his hips. "He won't be troubling you again."

I stiffened. "What does that mean? What have you done with him?"

"Sent him down!" He laughed.

I went mad. We struggled as I demanded he release Delmontre from that hellish place.

He thrust me from him. "If you want him so much, Kane, then go to hell and get him!"

He stalked off. I never dreamed he'd react like that over a servant. I was not relishing a trip to the underworld. I had no authority there. Kanaloa ruled that place. But I couldn't leave Del below with the demons.

So I prepared, thinking of enlisting the help of Ku, the god of war, to be of assistance, but I knew he wouldn't want to get in the middle of a dispute between Kanaloa and myself.

I never got to the underworld. I don't even know if Delmontre was ever there or if it had been a trap in waiting. As I went to leave the chambers, I felt the walls close around me. I used my powers to open a path but the walls closed again and there, within those walls, were two beings. One I recognised, an old woman that Kanaloa kept close to him, acting as his advisor. She practiced magic, and in her eyes were slithering snakes, her hair falling over her wrinkled face in clumps of dead leaves. I was always wary of her.

I'd always gone out of my way to avoid her, but suddenly she was right in front of me. At her side was what looked like a man but he had huge, razor-sharp teeth and blood red eyes. The old crone laughed as she moved closer to me. I inched along the suffocating walls, suddenly coming to the end. There was no place for me to go.

His teeth dripped, his bloody eyes glowed as he ran his long, jagged nails ran down my chest. "A beautiful gift before the end." He hissed. "Praise Kanaloa."

I let out a shout, feeling I could escape, but the old crone reached out and held me, those snakes blinding me. The creature opened his jaw. I felt the long, sharp teeth like nails sink into my flesh. The words of the old witch resonated in my head. "You will be forever cursed to roam the night, Kane, known to man as Malakai, thirsting for blood, never to see the sun. No longer god…now a beast, scraping the bowels of the earth… Go in pain!"

I woke up, lying on a deserted stretch of beach, with hideous laughter in my head. And something else – a thirst. A thirst for human blood. I don't know what I would have done without Felix. At that time before the war, he was a whole man who'd been my faithful servant for as long as I could remember.

Felix stroked my hair and talked gently to me.

"What… Where am I? What happened?" I knew I was in the human world. I knew something about me was different.

"Kanaloa cast you out. He sent me along to attend to you. He has made a case before the council that you can no longer rule due to your mysterious…affliction." Felix looked down at the sand.

"What affliction?" I asked, looking at the moon.

"You are…different. You are Malakai. You will thirst for human blood, walk the earth."

"He can't do this to me!" I roared. The earth rumbled with me. "I still have power."

"Yes," Felix said, "You have power, but you have been banned from that world. You are not recognisable to the immortals. You have been renamed as Malakai, no longer god of the forest and trees. He has approval from the council. They will back him."

"Delmontre," I said, looking at Felix. "We must save him from Kanaloa."

"And I will fight at your side, Kane. But know this – I don't believe Delmontre is to be trusted."

"How can you say that?" I demanded. "He loves me."

Felix looked away. "Of course he does."

I dug my hand into my pocket and found the shell, the one that would take us across the divide to our world. I threw it in the water and the ship appeared. I knew from the darkening skies it would not be an easy journey. Nothing would be easy from this time on.

As the waves roared around us, I navigated the ship to the shores of the immortals. There, I met with an army of demons and monsters. I shouted out for obedience but as Felix had said, they no longer recognised me as Kane.

We fought on until I came face to face with Kanaloa, his arms akimbo, with no sign of mercy on his face. He put up his hand and the warriors around him froze like statues. I wiped the sweat and blood from my forehead, my sword raised, ready to forge on. All I could think of was Delmontre, and how I had to save him.

For a while, there was silence. Kanaloa just looked at me with something akin to pity settling on his handsome face. I could abide his wrath, but not his pity. I would have moved forward to strike him if he hadn't chosen that moment to speak.

"The great vampire god, Luka, gave his existence as sacrifice to visit this curse upon you," his voice rang out clear and strong.

"Luka?" I echoed. I knew of whom he spoke. Luka was the last known surviving vampire, all-powerful, almost as *powerful as the gods.* "Why? Why would he make a sacrifice to you to curse me? I never harmed him."

He shrugged. "Perhaps he could no longer go on." His head shot up. "I have the approval of the council in this. No one here will help you, Malakai. I will give you five minutes to leave then I will banish that ship and abandon you to their mercy." He waved his hands around.

"You cannot banish my ship. And I still have power. You haven't taken it."

"Yes" — he smiled — "but unfortunately, Malakai, your power is of no use if not acknowledged."

"The crime I have done has been done in the name of love. Surely it is not that grave. I want Delmontre. Only then I shall leave."

Kanaloa laughed. "Shouldn't that be up to him?"

I narrowed my eyes, took a step. Felix placed a hand on my arm to caution me.

"Let's ask him, shall we?" Kanaloa turned and Delmontre walked out and stood beside him. He wore one of Kanaloa's finest robes.

I shook my head. "I…I don't understand. Del" — I glanced at him — "are you all right?"

He nodded. "I'm fine."

"What are you doing? What's going on? I came back for you…to save you from…" I trailed off.

"Let me explain," Kanaloa interjected. He placed an arm around my mortal lover and hugged him. "Delmontre has decided to stay with a winner. He is not interested in squandering time with a loser like you, an outcast, a cursed, wretched, has-been of a god."

"Del?" I sought his gaze. He looked away.

"Tell him, my love," Kanaloa urged my lover.

Del glanced up. "I am with Kanaloa now," he said, looking me square in the face. "I will be a god like him, and I…I no longer need you."

A knife in my heart, that's what it felt like. In that moment, I knew I'd lost everything.

"There is a way, Malakai," Kanaloa announced. "I am prepared to give you back your status and even share Delmontre."

I narrowed my eyes.

"I will forgive you. You may come back to my bed, to your world, if you submit to me in all things. The three of us" — he looked at Delmontre — "will be so happy together and — "

He never finished. I lunged for him, thinking if I got Del as well, it would be a bonus. But as I did, Kanaloa got hold of Felix. I chased after Kanaloa as he flew towards the volcano, Felix on his back.

The closer we got to the volcano, the hotter it became. My eyes and throat choked with volcanic ash as I tried to grab Felix. Kanaloa let out a laugh and flung Felix forward. Felix hovered over the volcano, screaming as I swooped up in the air and grabbed him. But it was too late. When I pulled him out Felix was near death, his legs completely gone.

I leaned over him and bit into my own flesh. I held my bleeding wrist to his mouth and forced the blood in. Then I sealed the bleeding pulp that was his bottom half so that he wouldn't bleed to death.

I picked him up in my arms and carried him back to the ship, surprised Kanaloa hadn't ordered his monsters to attack. On board, Kanaloa spoke to me, although he didn't show his face. "I am so disappointed in you, Malakai. I can't believe you are being so stubborn. We could be happy together."

"You got what you wanted. You wanted to hurt me. You have done it." I cried out. "And don't call me Malakai!"

As we sailed, Felix opened his eyes. He glanced down at himself and screamed over and over again. His screams stretched across the water and filled the skies. I plunked down on the deck and yearned to join him. Headed to the human world, doomed to wander the night, I would bide my time, waiting for the day I would return to claim my rightful place. I couldn't believe the council would abide this, leaving humanity in the hands of Kanaloa and my backstabbing mortal lover. But obviously Kanaloa had them all in his power, and now that power was a monopoly.

I moved over to Felix and pulled him against me, rocking him like a child, quieting his eternal sobbing. "Don't despair, Felix," I told him. "I will take care of you. You will be well again. And one day, I will take care of Kanaloa and his ambitious little whore."

"Kane," Felix said weakly, "Del…"

I put up my hand. "Do me one favour. Never mention his name in my presence again. He is dead to me."

Felix nodded. "As you like. Malakai?"

I gave him a look.

"I mean Kane. It's just that I can't call you Kane in the mortal world."

"Mortal world…" I let that settle on my tongue as the ship slipped through the portal into the other side. "Very well. Malakai it is," I said with a heavy heart. "What did you want to say?"

"How will I walk, get around like this?"

"If I could save you, I can help mend you somehow. Away from Kanaloa, I have some of my powers back. I will give you the power of levitation, and you won't need legs. Fear not, Felix."

"How could I fear with you at my side? But I grieve for you, master, for the betrayal. You loved him so."

It was true. I had. And Kanaloa, I knew down deep, had cared for me, but his feelings were fraught with possessive jealousy. I couldn't belong to just him, and that was where we differed. I wanted to be free to love and yet to love a mortal was the worst of all offences in Kanaloa's mind. That was why the council didn't intervene in my fate. Well, to hell with them.

Little did I know as I floated on that great water that Delmontre had never been the great love of my life. It was Jepoi, whom I'd yet to meet. And ironically, it was Kanaloa's punishment that was about to ensure our paths crossed very soon.

Chapter One

Hilo, the Big Island of Hawaii, Present Day

The volcanic eruption had taken everyone by surprise. Me, I saw it from the air flying back from taking a cardiac arrest patient to Honolulu. My flight partner, Jon, and I stared out of the window at the spectacular display, fire and angry molten lava shooting to the sky and back down to the sea.

"This isn't a small one!" our pilot, Alex, shouted from the cockpit. He angled back around so we could get another look.

"Check that out!" Alex called out at the exact same moment Kilauea Volcano's burning cauldron spewed fresh fire into the air. All three of us let out whoops of stunned excitement as flames accompanied the black river now moving fast along the trails that people normally walked.

Madame Pele, Goddess of the Volcanoes, was pissed about something.

In spite of the eruption, we were still able to land. Simple things like breathing and driving were a different story.

Jon and I had driven in my car to Hilo airport when we'd received the medical alert. He was too scared to head home with me.

"I'm staying right here," he insisted.

Not only did I want to go home, I wanted to get close to the fire. I'd never seen an eruption before though I'd hiked the volcano numerous times.

In the haze of the vog, the thick volcanic fog enveloping this side of the island, I made slow progress. It was so hard to breathe I knew it had been a mistake to come out here. I should have waited.

I did not want to become one of my own airlifted patients, so I pulled over to the side of the road. Out of nowhere, a small animal appeared.

Wait. No. I peered through the front windshield. It looked like a man. Except he had no legs and he was wearing a strange fur coat.

I immediately got out of the car thinking he'd been hit. I was a nurse. What if he needed help?

When I jumped out and called, "Are you okay?" the man scurried away. Almost seemed to levitate.

Oh, great. Now I'm hallucinating.

I tried following him. The air smelt like rotten eggs. The sulphuric gases burned my eyes, particles of lava hardening on my skin, even my eyelashes. I was afraid the higher I went on that mountainous road, the more likely the lava was to envelop me, as it had countless trees in previous eruptions.

From somewhere above, I heard the whine of helicopter blades. A dog barking nearby. Legend has it that the Goddess Pele, when she assumes human form, is either a gorgeous, young raven-haired temptress, or an elderly, frail old woman. And she is often accompanied by a small white dog.

Back towards Hilo, came the sound of ambulance sirens. I stopped and checked my cell phone. I had a signal but no text. I wasn't required to leap into action. One more look around for the legless man and I'd get back to my car.

Then, out of the relentless smoke, a man appeared. Oh, my. He was handsome. Dark-haired.

"What are you doing out here?" I asked. Good God he was a specimen.

"I might ask you the same question, Jepoi."

"I'm looking for a legless man."

"I happen to have both my legs." He smiled at me. "Will I do?"

* * * *

"So how bad was the date, Jepoi?" Evelin asked as I stood beside her at the kitchen sink.

"Hmm?" I came back to earth with a soft landing. Just thinking about the moment I'd met Malakai twenty-four hours ago made me feel all gooey inside.

"You've got a funny look on your face," she said.

"It wasn't bad. Far from it. In fact, it was the best first date I've ever had."

"I was kidding. I heard the furtive making out that went on all night. Made me want to take a cold shower. *And* smoke a cigarette. And I don't even smoke!"

Evelin made me laugh.

"Of course, being a Libra, I couldn't decide which to do first. The shower or the smoke so I gave up and just...diddled myself in bed."

Oh, too much information. I tried to keep busy, shelling the peas we'd just pulled from the garden. It was a little after seven a.m. and I hadn't even been to bed yet. Not like me. Not like me *at all*.

I didn't want to talk about Malakai. Not after the amazing date we'd had last night…when I'd done the unthinkable and spent all night in his arms on the back *lanai* cuddling and kissing him. I never did that on a first date… Come to think of it, I couldn't remember the last time I'd spent all night just making out. And this, in spite of the thick vog that still clung to the air from Kilauea's little crater party. In spite of the thirty mile distance, the smell, the tiny particles of lava that had continued to invade my skin, eyes, even my tongue.

Malakai had taken it all away with his erotic kisses.

Auwe, as we say in the islands. I already had it bad for the man.

I'd never had such an amazing date. He'd left at dawn and taken my heart, my mind, one of my socks and all my senses with him.

Outside the window, I spotted the kaleidoscope of Monarch butterflies before she did. Hilo's early morning rainfall had cleared the vog. The air no longer smelt of rotten eggs, and the skies had shifted from black-grey to a hopeful blue-grey.

"Huh," Evelin said, when I didn't respond. "I couldn't tell if it ended well or not. You're so quiet today. Usually I get all the gory details. Did you go all the way or just hover around all the bases?"

"Don't talk about him like that," I snapped before I could censor myself.

She looked up at me with some astonishment. "You really like this guy."

I glanced out of the window and saw her beloved butterflies doing a breathtaking aerial show in the lush, tropical garden. Our backyard was paradise, a sharp contrast with the front.

To see that side of it, one would think Evelin and I lived in a dump, but this was the way of almost everyone who lived in the 'real' neighbourhood of Hilo. Far from the towering hotel resorts hugging the shoreline, most residents kept to the upcountry slopes. I'd been renting a room in Evelin's house on Lihikai Road for over a year and the sight of the exterior had almost kept me from knocking on her door the first time I'd seen it. I understood the wisdom now and resisted my desire to weed the front yard and give the *lanai* a fresh lick of paint.

It was the island way. The *real* island way. Never outwardly show you have means. It discourages strangers from wanting things of you. I'd discovered after a lifetime of living on Oahu that most people on these outer islands didn't want to be bothered by people. They wanted to be left alone. And, unfortunately, hordes of tourists found their way here and many lingered. Most of them were anti-social dopers. Even the rich ones. Most were poor, dumped here with one-way tickets from mainland jails after doing time for petty crimes. Another reason we all went out of our way to prevent them from thinking we had anything of value to steal.

Backyards were a different story. Our backyards were our Shangri-la. I'd been nervous inviting Malakai here after a wonderful evening of dinner and music, but he hadn't looked askance at the ramshackle entrance. He'd looked beyond it and had won me the moment he'd bent to pick up a gecko from the creaky front steps before he could involuntarily tread on it.

"Tell me, about him, Jepoi," Evelin said.

"He took me to the craziest restaurant I've ever been to in my life," I blurted.

"Really? Which one?"

"I don't know."

"You don't know?"

"It sounds weird, but he said it was a private restaurant. Limited seating." Very limited. I couldn't recall seeing any other diners there. "They don't advertise." I stopped talking, remembering the first moment he'd fed me with his fingers.

"You know, those kinds of places used to exist here. I had no idea they were making a comeback. What did you eat? What's he like? Hotter than Asher?"

Where do I start? It sounds so clichéd. Tall, dark, handsome. Long black hair, piercing blue eyes that make me want to get naked. Malakai wasn't Asher. For the first time in months, the agony of his loss had begun to dim.

"Jepoi?" she prompted, her gaze turning in the direction of my pointed finger. Her mouth slackened to an appreciative *O*. She adored butterflies. They in turn were drawn to her. Evelin had taught me that a group of butterflies was called a kaleidoscope, a beautiful word for such gorgeous creatures. She laid down the pea pod in her hand and went outside. I stayed stock-still watching as she stood in the middle of the backyard, arms outstretched, the butterflies landing on her limbs. I'd read that Monarch butterflies were rare in the Hawaiian islands but it didn't surprise me that they would come to Evelin's house. An artist, almost all her images were of butterflies.

I snapped a few photos with my camera phone. I was out of space. I'd spent all the previous day shooting images of Kilauea's beautiful destruction.

The eruption had embarrassed the volcanologists who hadn't predicted it. Nobody could have predicted I'd meet Malakai. That was the moment when life for me changed. The moment I'd found hope again.

I still wondered what he'd been doing in the middle of that hot wreckage of trees covered in still-smouldering lava. He seemed so serene, so happy in the midst of the lonely wreckage.

He'd accepted my offer of a ride home. He directed me to his remote but interesting looking ranch-style house on the edge of a cliff. Funny that I'd never noticed it before.

Malakai had a deep, rumbling voice and a seductive smile I'd never get tired of, I was certain. He had a stillness that sort of reminded me of Evelin. I say *sort of* because something told me Malakai was far from the sedate, serene being he projected.

Evelin still stood in the garden and I watched as closely as I could without startling the butterflies. The fatal mating dance began. The male Monarchs took down the females and began their frantic copulation on the ground. I'd learned from Evelin that though it was a beautiful sight, the males often died after a vigorous session.

Cycles of love and death so closely entwined hurt my eyes. And my heart. Two butterflies landed on the windowsill. I watched their feverish dance and wished I could warn the male.

Run!

But I was convinced that like his human counterparts, the male butterfly would only be lured more strongly by the potency of a partner that could kill him as sweetly as she took his seed.

My cell phone rang and I took the call as soon as I saw it was from dispatch. Otherwise I'd be heading for bed. A guest of the Hilo Village Hotel exhibited symptoms of a raging fever and the hotel doctor was worried.

"He has stomach cramps and he's on his honeymoon. We need to airlift him to Honolulu," the operator said. "You and Jon are to meet the patient in the parking lot. He's with his wife. She's apparently not feeling so good, either."

"I'm on my way." Jon was my partner. On our fixed wing air ambulance service, the fully equipped medical flights always had two paramedics on board, plus the lone pilot.

"How long?" the operator asked. I could hear him typing all this into the system.

My job with Hawaii Air Patrol is what brought me to this island. I'm one of six paramedics trained to help people being airlifted to hospitals in either Maui or Honolulu. Most visitors to our islands have no idea that once they leave the populated confines of Oahu, on the outer islands they're in serious trouble in a medical emergency. Though there are small medical facilities in these places, they're not equipped for dire life-threatening situations. They're not even capable of dealing with difficult pregnancies.

That's where I come in.

"Ten minutes," I said, mentally getting dressed and preparing my kit. My uniform was a zippered jumpsuit affair that went over whatever I was wearing. My kit was propped up in the hallway awaiting my attention since I was on-call for four days out of five. I thanked the heavens and that pesky volcano goddess that the skies had cleared enough for me to make it in a timely manner.

As I ended the call, I stared at the two mating butterflies on the windowsill. I peered as closely as I could without frightening them. Now this I'd never seen before. The pair's wings flapped in unison and suddenly stopped. They had both died.

I shook my head. Sex and death. Love is forever. Wow…

My cell phone rang again. My grin widened so much it threatened to slide right off my face.

Malakai.

I had his number loaded into my phone already. I took the call, the first rumblings of his incredibly sexy voice making my cock grow hard on the spot.

"Good morning, beautiful," he said.

"Good morning." I could hardly speak I was so happy. I shook off my romantic haze. "I have an emergency call, I have to take it."

"I wish you wouldn't."

"What?" I was so shocked I almost laughed. Was he suggesting that I skip work? "It's an emergency," I repeated. "I have to take it."

"I have a bad feeling about this one," he said.

And here was the thing. Malakai was tall, dark, handsome, and absolutely spooky. He knew what I was thinking. He could read my mind, judging by the way he'd ordered food for me over dinner. He knew how to kiss and touch me for maximum impact.

Now he had a bad feeling about the call? Suddenly I understood. Air turbulence. The last twenty-four hours had been rough, the winds so severe it had brought the volcanic drift all the way to the ocean.

"The skies are clear. I'll be fine. Honest."

A significant pause on the other end of the line. "Well, if you're sure…"

"I'm sure. I gotta go."

"Do you wear gloves when you're working?"

"Not as a rule, no. Sweetie, I have to go."

"Can I see you tonight?"

"Yes." I added, "Please."

"Call me when you're back and please think about the gloves."

"Okay. I will." How sweet he was to worry about me, but I wouldn't be donning gloves. They weren't company policy. My boss, Kimo, liked the *aloha* touch, skin on skin.

I couldn't alert Evelin who was busy acting as a human bedpost for her butterflies that I'd received a work call. I scrawled her a note, then called my partner. I hurried into the bathroom where I ran a toothbrush across my teeth as I waited for Jon to pick up.

"Tell me that's an electric toothbrush I hear and not a vibrator," he said when he answered his phone.

"Toothbrush," I mumbled around the foaming paste in my mouth.

"Just as well. How was the date last night?"

"Fabulous." I swilled some mouthwash.

"Did you know it's illegal to have sexual relations with a porcupine in Florida?" he asked.

Jon was always coming out with crazy shit like this. I sure hoped he hadn't been up all night smoking *pakalolo*. Not when we had a call.

"I'll keep it in mind," I said.

My hands shook as I suddenly recalled the way Malakai had kissed my face. He had licked my ear until I actually came in my pants. I shook the thought out of my brain. No time for that that now.

"You drivin' to me?" Jon asked. I wanted to roll my eyes. He had the medic van. It wouldn't hurt him to drive a few blocks to me. My silence must have said it all.

"Wait outside," he grumped. Clearly, somebody hadn't got some last night.

In my room, I rolled deodorant across my pits and pulled up my jumpsuit, then shoved my feet into socks and sneakers. I was outside waiting for him, with seconds to spare. My cell phone rang. It was the hotel doctor. I knew Doctor Li pretty well and respected him. Most hotels had a subscription service with our company. The smaller bed and breakfasts usually didn't. Not that it mattered. We Hawaiians took care of our visitors. Always have. Always will.

Doctor Li was worried about his patient's escalating temperature. As Jon avoided hitting a peacock on the recently paved road, I listened calmly and made notations on my iPad. Doctor Li had e-mailed me his report and I checked the stats. Both the van and our plane were equipped with WiFi, which enabled me to begin processing our passengers for emergency check-in at Queen's Hospital in Honolulu.

"I have your report," I told Doctor Li. "You mentioned his wife doesn't feel well either."

"Yes. They came here from Texas for their second honeymoon. Married twenty-five years. She told me they'd both experienced flu-like symptoms before they arrived on island, but they'd already booked and paid for everything. They had dinner last night in the hotel but woke up this morning feeling terrible."

On island was hotel lingo. I could tell Doctor Li was worried. One sick client was bad, two was a PR catastrophe.

I could see from the report that the husband's temperature had spiked from one hundred and three point three to one hundred and four after Doctor Li had first been asked to examine the couple.

Very high, obviously.

"We have the patient ready for transportation," Doctor Li said.

"Very good. We're just pulling into the parking lot now."

Jon angled the van into the hotel's semi-circular driveway where one of our gurneys had been loaded up with what looked like a heavy-set man. Doctor Li stood beside him with one of the security officers and a woman, I assumed the patient's wife. She shifted her weight from one foot to the other looking distraught. I took charge immediately, jumping out of the van as soon as Jon had switched off the engine.

"Good morning, Doctor Li. Mrs Anderson, my name is Jepoi. My partner Jon and I will be escorting you all the way to Honolulu."

She nodded at me, her eyes great, big, round saucers of fear.

"I hate small planes," she said, her face flushed. Whatever her husband had, she most likely had it too. Since the couple had told Doctor Li that they hadn't been up to par before they'd arrived in Hilo, we had to assume they had contracted a virus back home. It was unlikely theirs was a food-borne illness.

Jon and I loaded the gurney into the van. Mrs Anderson and I climbed in beside the patient and I began checking his vital stats as Doctor Li waved us goodbye. I could tell he was relieved we'd taken over.

Mr Anderson was so feverish he was out of it. His red face and sweaty brow concerned me. His head went back and forth as I used a forehead swipe to check his temperature. One hundred and three. It had gone down a point since he'd last been checked. I immediately placed an oxygen mask over his mouth and nose to help his laboured breathing.

"What are you doing?" his frightened wife shouted. I was used to explaining to patients what I was doing every step of the way but sometimes their nearest and dearest proved to be harder to calm down.

"I'm just giving him a little oxygen." I contacted the hospital by radio, reporting the patient's blood pressure, which was high. I was so focused on Mr Anderson that I hadn't even noticed that Jon had driven us to the Hilo Airport where our tiny plane awaited us. We parked right on the runway outside our office located to the side. We left the van next to the building. Alex, our pilot for the day, already had the plane prepped. He ran to the back door and helped me and Jon remove Mr Anderson, wheeling the gurney to the plane's side. We got the gurney in, Jon helping Mrs Anderson aboard.

The plane had a few passenger seats but a cavernous space in the middle, enabling us to secure the folded gurney to the plane's sides. Mrs Anderson sat down, watching anxiously as we placed straps around the gurney to ensure her husband was jolted as little as possible.

Alex closed the doors and got into the pilot's seat. "Winds are fair," he announced as he started the plane. "We should be A-okay to arrive in Honolulu in fifty-nine minutes."

"Thanks," Jon said. He positioned himself at Mr Anderson's head, where he could closely follow the machine readouts as well as the chart we'd prepared for our patient. Doctor Li had contacted Mr Anderson's primary physician back home so we had his medical history on hand. He seemed very healthy, apparently up until now.

I remained beside the man who was moaning. We had no idea exactly what kind of illness he had but kept a check on his blood pressure and temperature, all of his stats available on a computer readout. His levels were very high, not surprising with the fever he had coursing through his body.

"Am I going to die?" Mr Anderson's watery eyes gazed up at me.

"No. We're going to get you to the hospital as soon as we can. You're going to be fine."

I hoped my words weren't a lie, but it was my job to reassure our patients. The last thing we needed was for them to freak out in mid-air. I secured all the straps fastening him to the side of the plane. He kept groaning with each movement of the craft.

Putting a comforting hand on his belly, I asked, "Are you in pain?" at the same moment his panicky wife asked, "Is he all right?"

The plane took to the skies and with it, Mr Anderson's temperature soared.

Mr Anderson yelped, but I didn't think the take-off had caused him any pain. I thought he'd been feeling bad for hours.

"Where does it hurt?" I asked him.

"Everywhere." He kept whimpering. "My whole body is in agony, but my stomach really hurts. I think I'm going to be sick."

Heat radiated from his prone form, his eyes glittering from his high temperature. It wasn't uncommon for a fever-induced illness to make a patient feel as if every bone in their body ached.

I alerted the hospital staff via my iPad and the doctor on call gave me permission to administer some pain medication to my patient to ease his suffering. This would also lower his temperature and hopefully help reduce his blood pressure. I couldn't allow him too much medicine however, because we needed to keep him conscious to communicate with him.

"I'm going to give you something for the pain," I told him, as I prepped a vein in his arm for the sterile solution the emergency room staff asked me to dispense, as well as ten ccs of Tramadol.

"What are you doing to him?" his wife shrieked.

The plane gave a lurch and I locked glances with Jon who took over caring for her as I handled Mr Anderson. My patient was frightened and the pain seemed to be worsening. I kept up a constant refrain of "You're doing great," as our pilot dealt with a spiralled patch of turbulence.

"Oh, my God!" Mr Anderson began to shake. I put another blanket over him, genuinely concerned when his temperature spiked at one hundred and four. One hundred and five was considered potential stroke level. I begged him to relax and trust me. His blood pressure zoomed up and I was afraid he really would stroke out.

Mr Anderson began to listen to me. His temperature stayed at one hundred and four and he closed his eyes. I knew the pain medication had begun to work and he drifted off again. His blood pressure dropped a little. His eyes opened again.

"Are we there yet?" His glassy gaze fell on me.

His wife began to cry. "How long is it going to take?" she begged.

"Another forty minutes," Jon told her, talking to her in soothing tones. He assured her we were doing everything possible for her husband. We hit a bumpy air pocket and the pilot caught my gaze as he flicked a glance over his shoulder. He gave me a thumbs-up.

"Ow, ow," Mr Anderson whined.

Dealing with two fussy, feverish passengers was no fun. I gave our patient a little more pain meds when he complained of a bad headache and his neck hurting. His stats were level, so I went easy on the amount I allowed him, but it worked. He relaxed, his breathing even, his hearing tuned into my voice. I'd entered a zone with him. I was his passageway between life and death.

I kept up a constant stream of conversation with him. I asked about his kids. When he mentioned his grandchildren his blood pressure dropped. He smiled when he talked about them and his dog, Buddy.

"Will I see them again?" he asked.

"Of course," I assured him. "And I expect photos at Christmas. I adore photos of children and dogs." He gave me a tremor of a smile. I kept him comfortable and calm and Jon did wonders with Mrs Anderson who'd stopped going berserk with every lurch of the plane. Ten minutes out of Honolulu, she shrieked, "There's Diamond Head! Oh my God! I want to kiss the ground when we get out. I never want to see the Big Island again as long as I live."

"My stomach aches real bad," her husband muttered. "And—" His voice broke off.

"And what?" I asked, trying to keep my tone gentle as the plane began to descend.

"My groin," he said. "I've never experienced pain like this. I hope it's not another hernia."

We prepared for touchdown, Jon radioing to the Queen's Hospital ambulance that was already driving across the tarmac to us. Mr Anderson's temperature had levelled out at one hundred and two point five — still high but I was pleased. With a lot of good care from the fantastic staff about to take charge of him, I was certain he'd be okay.

Our landing was smooth and swift.

"You did it!" Mrs Anderson clutched my upper arm with purple-painted talons.

I did my best not to scream as they dug into my skin.

"Glad we could be of service," I said. She wouldn't let go of me even as the engine died and we began to unfasten the safety straps around her husband.

"Thank you," he croaked.

Jon and I helped wheel his gurney to the ambulance, handed over our chart, then took turns hugging Mrs Anderson goodbye. She climbed into the back of the vehicle.

"Aloha!" she kept calling out.

Her poor husband had started moaning again.

"What if she's contagious?" Jon muttered as we waved the ambulance goodbye.

"Then, I guess we got what they got," I said cheerily. An involuntary shiver ran through me when I thought about my conversation with Malakai and how he'd asked me to wear gloves.

We left the pilot to deal with getting ready for our return flight to the Big Island and strolled into the small building that housed our company's on-site headquarters. We both took some time washing our hands and faces with the icky anti-bacterial soap in the men's room before we returned to the front counter.

Two men stood behind the desk, one working on his desktop computer, the other fiddling with the coffee machine. Kimo, a big, burly Hawaiian who'd started Hawaii Air Patrol, wore many hats for the company, everything from pilot to pit bull when it came to customer complaints.

He looked up and grinned at us, picking up the coffee carafe. "Two brews comin' at my two favourite bruddahs." Kimo was inclined to be cantankerous but had warmed up to me and Jon to a great degree since we'd so nicely played the token gays at his wife's recent baby shower. We'd gone halves on her most desired necessities—a Wild Life musical bouncy seat and a pair of glittery, ruby baby shoes from Pediped Originals.

We took Kimo's coffee cups and sat on the hard plastic chairs lining the wall. Above us, mounted high on a steel bracket, the TV was on. We watched a report about the latest volcanic eruption in the islands. The media trotted out the same depressing statistics with each eruption. A fresh-faced, terrified looking young woman in a bright yellow rain slicker was being bandied about by a fierce wind as she reported that ninety per cent of the islands' flowers came from the Big Island.

"Most of the islands' supply of our staple root vegetable, the *taro*, is also grown here and farmers say that all of the latest crops are ruined."

The scene flashed to rows and rows of exotic plants of flowers in commercial fields simply covered in black. The lava, once it erupted, became small hard dots that could be carried for miles by the wind. Impossible to remove, the results looked like a mass infestation of tiny black bugs.

"Record numbers of rental cars have been returned damaged beyond repair," the news reporter said from some windy outcrop near Kilauea, judging by the plumes of smoke behind her.

The scene cut to a row of rental cars lined up at Hilo Airport, all of them covered in the same black dots. Dang. The lava and had flown through the air, attaching itself to everything.

"Hey, maybe Steve can buy one of those cars. He won't give a shit about the lava," Jon said. I glanced away from the set and looked at him. He said this without a trace of sarcasm. He shrugged. "What? They always sell off ex-rental cars."

That was true. I picked my words carefully since we hadn't discussed Steve for a couple of weeks.

"He's back?"

Jon nodded. "Yeah. He's back."

I wanted to strangle Jon. I resisted the urge since I didn't want to go to jail. I wanted to be a free man for my date.

"How long's he been back?" I asked, trying to keep my tone neutral but even I could feel the chill in my voice.

"Thirteen days."

Hmmm…exactly around the time he stopped whining about him constantly.

"He says he's left his girlfriend for good this time. That he's ready to embrace his sexuality. He wants to come out."

Lemme guess. He just needs time.

"He says he just needs time." Jon fussed with his cell phone checking for texts.

I closed my eyes and pretended to fall asleep. Malakai was right there, waiting for me. As if beckoning me out of the shadows of my dreams, he stepped out from the steam created by the volcanic eruption. He was magnificent. Very Hawaiian. He took my breath away with his long, dark hair and lean, chiselled beauty.

"Good evening," he said.

I squeaked back a hello. I could barely speak when I saw him. He was dressed completely in black and at first I thought he might have been a priest, except he had no dog collar. His dark eyes bored into mine, making me feel hot all over. I thought it might have been volcanic heat, but it was him. He stared at me as if I were the only man in the world.

I'm not ugly. Not by a long shot. But I'm what they call *hapa-haole*, an island mix of Hawaiian, Thai, and Portuguese. My hair is short and I'm kinda skinny. Not a twink exactly, because I like my food too much, but at five feet, nine and a half inches, I felt like this gorgeous stranger towered over me.

"What are you doing out here?" he asked and like a moron I said, "I guess I came to find you."

He threw back his head and laughed.

My beautiful daydream was interrupted by Jon shaking me awake, not that I was asleep. I didn't mind going home, in fact I couldn't wait. I wondered what Malakai had in store for me this evening. I'd tried Googling the private restaurant he'd taken me to the night before but nothing had come up. I toyed with my cell phone looking at Google Maps. The road it had been on didn't appear to have any kind of business on it. I shook my head. He was a man of so many secrets, for sure.

On board the plane, I filed my reports and listened to Jon prattling on about his man. "I think we might go into business one day," he said.

That surprised me. He barely managed to make it to his job on time. How would he run a business of his own?

I tried not to smile thinking of the mysterious Malakai. He had invited me to dinner when I dropped him home and said the funniest thing I've ever heard from a date.

"I'm taking you somewhere special. A lovely restaurant, but you need to dress up. You must wear shoes and pants. Your best church *slippahs* are not good enough."

He'd made me laugh. Somehow he knew I was a bit of a shorts and sandals kinda guy out of my work uniform.

The restaurant he'd taken me to had been filled with gargoyles. Dimly lit, the place looked like a house and even now I could recall the scent of beeswax. Large candles had burned in wall sconces all around us.

In one small, cosy room, only an intimate, square table stood in it, and it had been set for two. Malakai had described the different gargoyles around us as our private waiter brought us food. The meal had been sumptuous, elegant. Unbelievable in fact. The tasting menu was like nothing I'd ever experienced. One course was called Ocean Cappuccino, a small but delicious dark soup of local lobster, shrimp and crab. The second course was a stunning piece of goat cheese from the Laughing Goat Dairy served with fried sage, red onion jam, and rare organic white honey that I could still taste on my tongue.

Malakai had hardly touched a bite. He'd sipped his wine and carefully avoided discussing himself except to say something interesting. Malakai told me he liked gargoyles because historically they were misunderstood.

"They are like vampires," he said. "They are said to be subdued by crucifixes, which of course, is ridiculous."

I'd been too overawed at the time to ask why. And I still had no idea how he knew my name when I'd met him. I'd asked him, but he'd looked blankly at me. I figured maybe I'd imagined it, the way I'd imagined the legless guy.

The comment about vampires and gargoyles intrigued me though. I would ask him more about that tonight.

As soon as I got home, I could tell something was different. Normally I would have thrown myself into bed but I could hear laughter. *Oh. My. God.*
Malakai.

I dumped my gear and made my way to the back part of the house. I felt a wave of crazed jealousy when I saw him drinking wine with Evelin. She'd thrown her head back, the better to display her long, golden hair and throaty laugh that worked so well with straight men. Maybe she thought she could sway him over to her team.

He lounged against the kitchen counter, a sexy, homo-erotic vision in his tight jeans and black shirt. He straightened, his whole face brightening when he saw me.

Evelin's eyes widened when he pulled me towards him by the collar of my jumpsuit. His mouth met mine in a kiss that almost left me whimpering and Evelin rendered speechless.

"I was going to take a shower," I said when he broke off the kiss. He gazed into my eyes and my cock went rigid.

"Let's go, Jepoi." He put his wine glass on the counter and led me out of the kitchen. Evelin said something, but I was lost to her words. I let Malakai lead me into my small bathroom where he shut the door behind us and began kissing me in the same, impassioned way, with his entire body, as he had on the *lanai* all night.

This time, he took my clothes off. And his. He ran the shower taps, my gaze glued to his massive cock. Oh, boy. Could I ever take that thing?

He drew me under the steamy water, soap and sponge following every kiss he put on my hot skin.

"How are you feeling, Jepoi?"

"I feel fine." The truth was I was feeling dizzy. He always did that to me. He kissed me, his lips moving to my collarbone, which he'd already discovered was a hot spot for me. I almost came but he suddenly turned off the taps.

"Hey!" I protested. "I was enjoying that." He dried me off. I was tired. So tired. He kept telling me I needed to rest. Oh, yes. I wanted to rest with his cock buried deep in my ass. He led me to my room and threw back the bed clothes. I climbed in, holding my arms out to him. Man it was hot. Had Evelin turned up the heat?

He leant down and kissed me. My brain had gone foggy. Why was he wearing clothes? Was he going somewhere? Oh, yes. We had a date.

"I'll be there," he said. At least I think he did. His voice seemed far away. I clawed at the space between us. Wanting him. Wanting us.

He seemed to hesitate when I begged. "Please," I said over and over again.

Malakai's lips brushed mine. Why was my mouth so dry? I felt his tongue swipe my lips and move down my body.

"Oh, suck me," I whispered. I held my breath as his mouth trailed down my belly and stopped at my groin. Reverent fingers strolled across it. Why was he being gentle with me? Oh, I longed for his tongue to prepare me for him, his huge cock to be in me. I panted as he lifted my legs, which suddenly seemed heavy. What was wrong with me?

He dropped his face, his mouth closing on my ball sac. I think I cried out as his lips tugged at the fragile skin, his fingers squeezing on the balls. He held them with a possessive grip. He looked up at me, his eyes ablaze as he lifted my ass to his face. I watched him lick and suck my hole.

The bliss was beyond anything I'd ever experienced. He really seemed to love what he was doing. He stabbed his tongue at me then his mouth claimed me once more. His fingers moved inside me, duelling over my hole with his tongue. I could feel it in me now and started to come. He replaced his tongue with his fingers, his mouth moving over my cockhead as I came, deep and hard into his throat.

My exhaustion overtook me and I closed my eyes, aware that my throat suddenly hurt. What was the matter with me? It seemed like seconds later that the lights came on and my bedroom was filled with people.

"Doctor Li?" I gaped at the hotel doctor. "What are you doing here?"

My God. There were two men with him wearing surgical masks.

"How do you feel, Jepoi?" he asked.

"Why does everyone keep asking me that?" I glanced at my bedside clock. Seven p.m. I had to get ready. I tried getting out of bed but my body wouldn't obey.

"Where's Malakai?" I thought I could see him in the mist. No. It was weird. I couldn't see straight. I felt like shit.

Fever.

"May I examine you, Jepoi?" he asked.

"What for?"

He drew the covers back and poked at my belly and groin. I almost shot out of bed.

"Yow!" I screamed. "What the fuck?"

"Jepoi, Jepoi, I'm very, *very* sorry to tell you that we have to put you in quarantine."

"Quarantine? Are you crazy? I don't have time for quarantine. I have a hot date!"

He leaned closer and I realised he had a mask on, too. He'd lifted it over his head to talk to me.

"I'm sorry to have to tell you like this but Mr and Mrs Anderson are very ill. He's at death's door and I'm afraid what they have is highly contagious and my boy, I think you've caught it."

"Caught what?" What the hell was going on? Why were they wearing gloves? Why could I hear Evelin crying?

"You have the lumps on your groin. Just like he did. Buboes."

"Oh, no, no, no," I said, shaking my head vehemently but even as I said the word over and over again it started to make sense. Holy fucking fuckity fuck.

He was telling me I had one of the most deadly diseases known to man.

I had the bubonic plague.

* * * *

The trip to Oahu almost broke my heart. Jon, Evelin, Alex, and I were all flown by a crew in hazmat suits and masks. I'd left a message for Malakai but when I begged the ground crew to make a stop at Malakai's house, they claimed there was no such residence.

"There's nothing on that ridge, Jepoi. Been nothing there for decades."

Evelin wouldn't stop sobbing and wouldn't look at me.

None of us had any words, any clue what the hell was going on until we reached Queen's Hospital. Kimo was on his way to a room of his own, pitching a fit at me. I had no idea why. It wasn't my fault. Then I realised I'd had the closest contact with the infected patient and anyone I'd come into contact with since then could be endangered. Plague spores travelled by air. Just breathing as they were around me could have contaminated them.

We were each placed in isolation units and the rotating medical staff came to see us every hour. I heard Mr Anderson and I were the worst. His wife was recovering nicely. As time wore on, how much time I had no idea because nobody would tell me, but I learned that neither Kimo nor Evelin had contracted the virus and had been allowed to return home.

But I became more and more sick, the hideous buboes covering almost my entire body. I heard Jon was pretty sick but was expected to recover. Why? I wondered. Why me? Why did I get it so badly?

My thoughts kept going to Malakai. He'd begged me not to fly. He'd begged me to wear gloves. Had he really been at the house? Had he bathed me and made love to me? I slipped in and out of consciousness as teams of doctors and nurses came to visit me. All were agog, simply fascinated by the resurrection of what we'd all thought was an ancient, extinct disease.

I wasn't happy when I learned that the Andersons had picked it up on their farm on the mainland. You could say I was downright bitter. Mainlanders, foreigners had been bringing incurable diseases to our islands for two centuries including the plague.

Everything old was new again.

Including my resistance to all the doctors' fancy remedies.

I wondered about death. Would it take long? Would I see rainbows and angels or would I just disappear and feel and see nothing? My people had always believed that seeing rainbows meant death was coming, either your own or someone close. I didn't see any being in my room with no windows and had only my troubled thoughts.

Late one night I felt I was leaving. My spirit seemed to leave my body then I heard a voice.

"Jepoi."

Tears filled my eyes. It was him.

"Malakai."

"I'm sorry I couldn't come sooner. So many protections on this building." He shook his head. "I hadn't expected that."

He looked different. Sadder. He gazed down at me. "I can save you, Jepoi. I want to save you. I have bargained with the underworld for your soul. I can save you, but they say I can't be with you. All these centuries and they still want to see me in torment."

I didn't understand. "What underworld? Or did you mean underwear?"

"Let me look at you."

"No. Oh, no. I'm hideous. You'll throw up." I clutched the bedding to my chin. I did *not* want him to see me covered in horrible pustules.

He didn't listen. He drew down the thin hospital bedding and gazed over my body with curiosity and infinite pity.

"Let me save you. Perhaps one day, we can love. Never doesn't have to be forever."

His mouth opened and fangs appeared. He turned my head and choked off my words with a single, stinging bite. He drank from me and I could feel him taking, yet giving. I began to feel light, peaceful. No more pain. My cock grew hard and I came.

And then...

He was gone.

With the shadow of light.

Chapter Two

The wind blew unusually hard across Oahu that night. I stood watching from the shore as the great waves lifted and floated then lifted again, as if bowing in homage to me. Felix was nervous but really, there was nothing I could do to calm his fears.

"Malakai, do you think he knows?" Felix twittered as he sat in the sand, pulling the grains into piles then scattering it over again.

I glanced at the deformed little man who dared not show his face to the world. Jepoi had seen him in the volcanic mist, but I think I'd managed to act as if he might have imagined it. Long ago, I'd saved Felix from being thrown into an active volcano and over the centuries, protected him from Kanaloa. Felix had shown his loyalty again and again. The little man was my only friend really, but at times, like at present, he had a tendency to play on my last nerve.

"If you mean Kanaloa, then yes, he knows." I glanced around me. "He knows everything."

"It's hard to believe the tribunal defied him as you claim."

No one would have dared question me like that except for Felix.

I lifted my shoulders nonchalantly. "It wouldn't be the first time now, would it?" I walked back inside. I'd been using this house as shelter, a house that could only be seen by those I chose. Not even Kanaloa could find it. And when I finally left here, it would disappear along with me.

Felix scrambled after me on his palms, what was left of his legs dragging. "Are you sure they approved, or did you just go ahead without asking?"

It was enough questioning now and Felix understood as I turned and fixed him with a cold, icy stare. I didn't have to get cross with him. I wouldn't anyway. I had pity for Felix, for what they'd done to him. And sadly, no matter what magic I'd summoned, I couldn't fix him. Even my blood, which gave him eternity, could never restore him to his former self. Only Kanaloa could undo the damage. And he wouldn't. At least I'd enabled Felix to levitate.

Felix didn't follow me as I walked into the bedroom and closed the door and I was grateful. I needed my solitude, to be alone with my thoughts. There was no sound as I lay on the bed. Complete silence. I thought of Jepoi, the sores which had spread over his beautiful body and I sighed heavily. Jepoi would have died if I hadn't given him my blood. I'd had to save him. I'd not connected with a mortal being like that for centuries. I'd not felt anything really, for such an achingly long time that being with Jepoi that night had come as a sudden breath of air, a delightful surprise. And yes, I'd pleaded my case before the underworld, made promises I probably wouldn't or couldn't keep, but none of that mattered.

Existence meant very little to me. I'd been here since the beginning. I had no fear of Kanaloa for myself, only for the threats he made against innocents on my behalf. There wasn't much he could do to me personally that he hadn't done already. I couldn't end it even if I was tired of wandering this earth with the idiotic curse he'd placed on me. I was as connected to the water, and the sky, to all living things, as Kanaloa was himself. And in spite of the fact that I'd lost control, there were some members of that tribunal who had sided with me over Kanaloa in the bad old days when the battle for heavens and earth raged. But I'd lost for reasons I didn't want to revisit at the moment. And in spite of that, it hadn't been enough for Kanaloa.

You hate me. Yet, you once loved me. We could rule together, side by side, our lust for each other as powerful as our lust for power.

But he was a god of vengeance and hate. He wanted death and war for mortals. It wasn't my vision at all. Then of course there was…no, I'd vowed never to say his name. He was lost forever to me.

I will have no part of your lust for power. You will not win this war.

But he had. Kanaloa had won the war by threatening to destroy the one I really loved, a lover who at the end, betrayed me for power and ended up in Kanaloa's bed.

Now, the world embraced greed and cruelty. Humans destroyed the earth and each other, and I, Malakai, once known as Kane, the ancestor of chiefs and the giver of life, was the bringer of death.

It wasn't enough that Kanaloa had emerged victorious and taken the one I loved, he'd cursed me for leaving, vowing I would walk the earth, never seeing daylight, living in darkness and craving the blood of those I sought to bring salvation and light to.

"I hate you, Kanaloa," I shouted in the dark room. "One day, no matter how long it takes, I will destroy you, and take my rightful place." But even as I said it, I knew it wouldn't be. He was still obsessed with my every move. He'd known I was going to save Jepoi, and he'd put barriers around the hospital to keep me out. But it hadn't stopped me. I still had some magic. He hadn't drained it all when he'd made me into this undead thing.

Now as I drifted, I wondered at my purpose for saving Jepoi. I was never to reveal my existence to mortals. If they discovered what I was, I was sworn to destroy them, and I struggled every waking hour not to hurt mortals in any way. Often I'd drink from them without them really knowing. As they slept, like a thief in the night, I'd enter their room and lean in, inhale their scent and drink what I needed.

They'd wake up a little tired but none the worse for wear. What was it about Jepoi that actually caused me to speak to him, make love to him, and allow him to remember it, well, most of it?

I blocked out the feeding part. But then most of the time, I made love to him, and it was as addictive as the blood. For a short time I fed then sealed the wounds on his throat with my saliva. He was walking around when I left, he hugged me goodbye. I left well before sunup. He seemed happy. I was pleased to render him so. He'd made me feel as I had before the transformation.

Now, the return of a disease that seemed primitive, punishing, pure evil as only Kanaloa could conjure. And the most painful part was that he was doing it for my benefit. *Why make innocents suffer?*

I knew one of them would be Jepoi. I suspected that Kanaloa had started the contagion so Jepoi would be afflicted. He had a cruel sense of humour, him and my former lover, whose name no one would ever force from me. My mouth twisted in bitterness as I thought of him. My only satisfaction was that he could never have me. He'd berated Kanaloa for letting me go, thinking that he could have ultimate power as Kanaloa's lover, and me for dessert. Victory, however, was bittersweet.

I rose as the sun went down again. Felix scampered close to me as I emerged. I stroked his hair lovingly and he rested his cheek against my thigh. I was the only source of comfort and affection he had. And until I braved that encounter with Jepoi, he was mine. "I will always be here for you," I told him.

"Kane," he whispered, one of the rare occasions he addressed me by my rightful name. "I love you, master."

I leaned over and kissed his head. "And I, you. Let us resume our chess game, shall we?"

Felix nodded with enthusiasm

The thunder crackled overhead. I smiled. That could only mean that Jepoi was safe and happy.

As I sat waiting for Felix to make his next move, my chin resting in my hand, I thought about checking on my mortal friend. I know I'd promised not to take him as a lover again, but that didn't prevent me from making sure he was okay. I glanced at Felix. "Are you planning to move that game piece tonight or next year?"

"I'm thinking."

I stood. "Keep thinking. I've got to go out. I'll be back."

"There is nourishment in the fridge," he said, still studying the chessboard.

"Leftovers," I scoffed and exited the house. My guess was that he still wouldn't have moved by the time I returned. This sometimes took days, and still I always won.

I smiled as I scouted a place to take off in the night sky. One time I'd let him win, for the hell of it. I was thinking of the pleasure that would bring to Felix as I walked up to the small house where Jepoi lived with the female Evelin, the one with all the butterflies.

She was on the front porch as I appeared. She was watering some flowers and came close to dropping the same jug she held in her hand.

"Oh, it's you," she said.

I lowered my head to her in respect. "Good evening, Evelin. I've come to ask after Jepoi. Is he feeling well?"

She walked down the steps, her gaze on my face. Mortals often seemed a bit transfixed by me. I simply needed to refocus them. "I heard he was ill."

"Yes, but…he's made a full recovery. Doctors were a little…baffled. He went to work and he's now out with his friends."

"Ah, well then." I prepared to leave. It was probably for the best.

"He's different now, doesn't need much sleep, all kinds of energy, it's like he…like the disease revitalised him. It didn't do the same to Jon, I hear."

I smiled. My blood had revitalised him. I'd given him just enough to boost his immune system to the max. He'd probably never so much as catch a cold. And it was possible he'd live to be one hundred or more. But for what he'd given me, that taste of paradise, of feeling something again, it was my way of repaying him.

"He'd love to see you," she was saying. "I know where he went."

I cocked my head. "Yes?" It wasn't a good idea but what the hell. I glanced up at the skies and smirked. *Fuck you, Kanaloa and Mr No Name!*

"He's with a group of guys on Carlsmith Beach Park. Not sure where but they're doing a camp fire and stuff. He used to be so beat after work now he's raring to go all the time. You know…"

She went on and I kind of tuned out. I bid her good night, and figured I'd pay Jepoi a visit, a short one. Hell, who was I kidding? I wanted that feeling again.

I went back to the house to change. Poor Felix was still considering his next move. He was so focused that I walked into the bedroom without him noticing. Black leather pants, dark purple silk shirt. That should do it. I smiled at my reflection. Thankfully Kanaloa had let me keep that, if only to remind me of what I couldn't have.

Yes, I'd been given physical beauty. Didn't do me much good, wasn't as if I could go out to attract a life mate or anything.

When I came out of the room, Felix's eyes widened. "You are a sight. Please tell me you're not going to see him again."

"Him has a name. It's Jepoi. I'm only going to make sure he is in good health."

"Right!" Felix snorted. "And I'm the king of Siam."

I bowed my head and grinned. "Greetings, Your Majesty. May I be excused from your royal presence?"

"Not amusing. Please, Malakai, don't go," he pleaded. "You could ignite something, a storm you wouldn't believe."

"To hell with Kanaloa."

"It's not just him. It's—"

54

I put up my hand. "Don't you dare!" I threatened. "You know better than to say his name in my presence."

"He still wants you. He regretted his decision, he begged you on his knees to take him back at the end."

"He betrayed me," I said, my heart going cold. "He thought he could have it all. But you can't. I'm living testimony to that. Felix," I softened my voice, "please...don't chastise me for checking on Jepoi. I promise you it will be for only a short time. I know it can't be forever. I wouldn't put his life in jeopardy. I would never do that."

Felix nodded. "I'm going to win this one," he said, examining the board.

I smiled slyly. "Perhaps."

Within minutes, I was walking along the beach. Carlsmith wasn't for tourists, it was for locals who appreciated the quiet lagoons and the turtles that were so tame they would swim right up to the snorkelers. I could see the bonfire in the distance, could even see Jepoi sitting around it with two others, laughing. My vision was sharper than humans'. I could have stayed at this distance where he would have never seen me, and just admired him, assuring myself he was all right. But I found myself compelled to move closer. Like a moth to the flame, I was drawn. *Only for a short while, Kane.*

And as I approached the three men, I wondered what they'd say if they knew who I'd been, and what I was now. They could never know of course, but it didn't stop me from entertaining the idea.

Jepoi jumped to his feet when he saw me, his expression animated. I could hear the thudding of his heart, the whooshing sound of blood moving through his arteries. I turned the volume down so I could hear the words he was saying instead.

"Malakai! How good to see you," Jepoi said, inching closer. "What are you doing here? How did you find me?"

The other men rose as well. I felt the warmth of their gazes moving over me, desire in their eyes. I lowered my head to them. "Good evening." I turned my attention back to Jepoi. "I came only to see if you were feeling better. I heard you were ill."

"Yes, I'm fine, better than fine." He glanced at his friends. "Do you mind if I take a walk with Malakai? I need to talk to him about something."

His two companions murmured their agreement but stared at us with envy as Jepoi took my arm and moved me away from the others. I enjoyed the possessive way he clutched my arm. "There's so much I want to say to you, ask you," Jepoi said.

We were some way from his friends now. I glanced down at him, smiled. "Yes?"

He placed his hands on my face. "You are incredibly beautiful," he breathed. "I feel weak being this close to you. Tell me you came to spend the night with me."

I took a step away. I glanced out at the water then up at the moon. The stars were twinkling in the sky. All was well. "I came to make sure you'd recovered."

"What did you do to me?" He searched my face.

"Nothing," I lied.

"You saved my life. I was dying. How did you do it?"

I shook my head. "You are strong. You did it yourself."

"You came to me." He paused. "Where is your house?"

"You know where my house is." I sucked in some of the cool air.

"It's not there anymore. Your house vanished like magic."

I smiled, touched his cheek. "The sickness. You hallucinate."

"I don't care where it is anyway. Stay with me," he pleaded.

I pulled him against me, rubbed my cheek against his hair. The hunger grew inside me and I could taste him, the rich, red blood flowing into my mouth, between my teeth. I wanted him naked. I wanted to touch him then sink my teeth into his flesh and drink.

He was feverishly kissing me and I felt the change, a change he couldn't see, he wouldn't understand. I released him and turned my back, recovering.

"Is there someone else?" he asked.

I wanted to laugh, or cry. Someone else! That was a joke. I turned around again, quite presentable and shook my head. "No one. Tell your friends good night, and we'll go somewhere quiet, just the two of us. Would you like that?"

He nodded.

"Okay, I'll wait for you."

He ran back to his friends, and a few minutes later, he was holding my hand. "Where are we going?"

"To that house you said didn't exist. We need to take a boat across the river."

"That's not where it was," he said, shaking his head.

I looked into his eyes. *Yes, it was. It was there. Accept it, love. And forget that I made you well. Remember only the pleasure I gave you with my body, and allow me to give it to you again, one last time.*

There was no more talk of the location of my house and he entered it, acting like it was the first time. I sent a stern message to Felix to make himself invisible, which he did.

I brought Jepoi to my room and closed the door. I noticed he was trembling with need. I wanted to make it good for him, but I reminded myself that he was a mortal. I had every intention of being gentle, but Jepoi had other ideas. As his mouth smothered mine, he grabbed a hold of my shirt with his hands and tore it open. His lips left mine to trail down my chest as he pulled the shirt from my back then his fingers were at my pants. He yanked down the zipper while he moved his tongue frantically over one nipple then the other.

I stroked his hair as he pulled my pants down to my knees and gripped my ass cheeks.

His lips went to my throat and I let my head go back as again Jepoi moved his mouth down to my chest where he licked and suckled my nipples before sinking to his knees. He took my cock in his fist, his gaze slanted upwards. Our eyes met and I watched his tongue dart out to taste me. He pressed my erection against his cheek for a moment, his other hand gripping my calf and squeezing.

I moved my fingers through his hair and Jepoi licked the length of my shaft. Then he ducked his head lower and took my balls in his mouth, suckling and licking until I felt my knees grow weak. He tongued at my shaft then around the head, teasing until my fingers tightened in his hair. I wanted to be in his mouth, feel his lips tighten around the shaft. Blessed pressure and release.

Again he looked up at me, and I hoped my eyes were normal and not glowing like some fiend. But he kept the eye contact as I watched his mouth open and he took the head of my cock into this mouth.

I closed my eyes, licked my lips as he took more and more of me, pushing his body against my open legs, his head back. My cock went deeper. I grabbed his hair now, yanked as he started to deep throat me, his tongue still working, cheeks filling with air. "Jepoi!" I cried out.

He clutched my ass cheek, one finger flirting along the crevice and I came. He slowly backed away, smiling, wiping at his mouth, and I slid back against the wall, my entire body pulsing from those precious seconds of release.

When I looked down, I saw that his chin and chest were covered with the results of his efforts. I held out my hand and brought him to his feet. We kissed deeply, and I was ready to repay his efforts. I was secure in the knowledge that he wouldn't be left wanting, and I forgot all about his mortality.

I lay him down on the bed, his mortal, thudding beauty giving me everything as I spread his legs and began to lick every inch of him. When I got to his cock, I took my time, fondling him and feasting on his succulent erection, moving my tongue slowly down his slick shaft, savouring the taste of him, the smell, which to me was even more fragrant.

I lifted his legs as he moaned and delved my tongue deep into his most private cavity, an invasion that brought the most pleasurable sounds from his lungs.

I smiled and flipped him over, inserting my fingers into him and finding that place that caused him to cry out my name. "Malakai!"

I longed to hear him say Kane but Malakai would do, especially since his pleasure was only heightening mine. I lifted him again to his knees, placed his hands on the wall. His back to me, I kissed across his shoulders, down his spine, again pumped him with three then four fingers. I forgot gentle, I forgot everything and for a time, I was again Kane, giving pleasure without limits. I gripped his hips, snaking my hand around to roughly handle his cock and balls. I teased him with my cock, jabbing his readied ass then withdrawing before sinking deep into his ass.

"Malakai, Gawd!"

Yes, I was a god. And I intended to fuck him like one. I seized his hips and delved into him, my forehead resting on his back. He cried out once then let his head go back, his body covered with sweat. "Fuck me. Fuck me!"

In an iron-like grip, I moved all the way to the hilt then out, then in, slowly, side to side, making him scream then finally, fucking him so hard and fast, the bed began to shake. I was sure we'd bring it down so I dragged Jepoi on the floor and took him, face down.

I heard his heart race at a frenzied pace and I slowed down before coming inside him. I feared he'd have a heart attack, which reminded me of the fact that Jepoi was mortal.

When I sat back, I pulled him with me. I was still hard, and I turned him so that he was straddling me. He looked at me in wonder, his expression a little dazed, his mouth opened. I spread his thighs over me and positioned my cock, bringing him down on it. He moaned long and hard and, placing one hand on my chest to steady him, he fucked himself on my cock while he teased his own nipple with the other.

I watched Jepoi as his tongue played around his lips in sensuous pleasure. He took my cock up inside him like a god would, greedily and with pure joy.

I reached out and toyed with his cock, erect again and straining for a few more seconds of glory. "Come for me," I coaxed.

His gaze met mine. "Your cock is so..." He moaned as I stroked him hard.

"Is so what, Jepoi?" My hand moved over his stomach and down to his cock again.

His head went back and as he came, he cried out, "Oh...yeah!"

I smiled. I lifted him off my cock and pressed him back to the floor. I kissed his mouth then moved to his throat. I had to have a taste. With that image of him moving on my cock in my head, I bit down into his flesh, taking only a little. It was ambrosia. He was ambrosia. I licked over it quickly as I heard him protest.

"Ouch. What was that?"

"Nothing. A little nibble," I said.

He was falling off to sleep and I sank my teeth into the tender flesh of his throat and drank his rich, warm elixir again as I stroked his cock.

Jepoi moaned and whimpered as his cock thickened again before he came in my hand. I licked the wounds on his neck and watched them heal instantly, teasing his lips with mine. I let him rest then before the night was through, I took him again, again giving him the roughness he'd enjoyed so much before. He screamed that name I'd come to accept as I took him on the floor, against the wall then again on the bed, pushing his head over the side and making him deep throat my cock again.

Finally, Jepoi collapsed in my arms, satiated and exhausted, taking more than any mortal without a boost from my blood could have taken. I wanted him to remember me, but little else, not the house, not the part where I'd saved him, just me.

Before he awoke, I picked him up in my arms and carried him back to the beach. The sun had yet to rise so I stayed with him, built a fire, watched the stars. He awoke soon after, reaching for me. "Malakai?"

I smiled at him, let him kiss me. It was good-bye. The sun would be up in minutes. I had to leave him. And I probably shouldn't meet him again.

I put him away from me after that kiss and stood. "I need to go now."

He looked confused. "But why? After we made love like that. My God, I've never been made love to like that before. Malakai, I love you."

Something caught in my throat. "No," I said. "You don't." I could see the beginnings of the sunrise at the horizon. "Good-bye, Jepoi." I hurried off, thinking I could take off quickly from behind a tree somewhere. Maybe I wasn't going to make it in time. Maybe that was a good thing. But I couldn't die. Even the sunlight wouldn't kill me. Although I'd suffer for it, smell my own flesh burn in the bright sunlight which was not an experience I was anticipating, but it would remind me of the pain in my heart. *Don't see him again.*

As it turned out, I made it to the house before the sun had fully risen. Felix was at the door, pulling me inside as if a wind might threaten to take me outside again. He was miffed at me. "What possessed you?"

I deserved it I supposed. "I'm fine. Don't make a fuss."

"You were with him. I smell that human all over you. Malakai, honestly!" He had his hands on his hips which made him look like a teapot.

I smiled and walked into the living room. I glanced at the chessboard. "You haven't moved yet?"

"Don't change the subject. You've been a naughty boy. We'll catch hell for this."

I laughed aloud. "Naughty boy, eh? There's a first." I thrust myself into a comfy chair and checked my hands. No charred flesh. Too bad.

"I've thought it often but kept my tongue. But honestly, Malakai, you have become quite restless. Why not leave this place, find another?" He turned to look at the fireplace.

My eyes narrowed. I sat up. "Why? Have you heard something?"

It was not unlike someone I refused to name to communicate with Felix. I feared he thought Felix sympathetic to his plight.

"Felix!" My voice almost shook the rafters.

"He says he intercepted your dreams."

"What?" I stood. "How dare he do that to me? Is nothing sacred anymore? He had no right to be in my dreams or...anywhere else."

"He saw him...your human...although he doesn't know if he's real or fiction."

"You didn't say anything, did you?" I met his gaze.

"Would I give you away? No, I lied of course. I told him you have had no contact with any mortal named Jepoi."

My eyes widened. "He knows his name?"

"He heard the name in your dream."

"Then he's been using the dream merchants. Does Kanaloa know?"

Felix shook his head. "Kanaloa is very jealous. If he knew...he...you know who...and why can't we say his friggin' name, Kane?"

"Malakai, and you know why. Go on...you said that this is being done behind Kanaloa's back."

Felix nodded. "Appears so. Malakai, have a heart, he's hurting. He's like a child and..."

"You let him charm you, he makes you pity him with his puppy dog eyes," I sneered.

"He's afraid of what Kanaloa has in store. He didn't approve of this old disease coming back. He told him to stop. I think we could coax him back, Malakai, maybe use him to help us, turn things around you know?"

"Bullshit!"

Felix's eyes widened. "Did you say—?"

"Yes, I said bullshit." I pointed at him. "You will tell him nothing except this for me. He is to stay the hell out of my dreams because if he doesn't, I will report him to the council, tell them that he's been using the dream merchants."

"Okay." Felix sighed.

"And how has he paid them?"

"I...I'm not sure." He looked down.

"Felix!"

"He's made promises."

"Promises about what?"

"Well, co-opted dreams of course. He has sold them one that...well...it hasn't materialised yet." Felix slid back up against the table and almost toppled the chessboard.

"Go on," I grunted, reaching out to steady the board.

"The one that's worth the most on the dream market...the one with...you and him and...you know who...Kanaloa!"

My jaw dropped. *That little bastard.* I'd flay him if the merchants didn't do it for me. "Who's he been dealing with?"

"Starzs."

I sighed. Felix had gifts and he was about to use them. "Get me in touch with him."

"Now?" Felix squeaked.

"Now."

Felix hobbled over to the chessboard. "Didn't even get to move," he muttered.

"You weren't going to bloody well move anyway. Now do it!"

Felix closed his eyes. A few minutes later, he spoke, the voice deeper, sounding far away. "Kane. A pleasure. What can I do for you?"

"You are being fucked."

"By you, my Lord? How delightful."

"Don't be ridiculous. You know what I speak of. You have no right to look inside my dreams. I've never sold my dreams to you."

"Pity. Bet they'd be very stimulating."

"You cannot grant access to my dreams. And what he promises you, will never be."

"He guarantees it. And besides, if he doesn't deliver—"

"If he doesn't deliver, what can you do about it? Are you going to take on Kanaloa himself? You know Kanaloa is totally unaware of all this."

Silence.

"Starzs!" I bellowed, enraged. "Don't you dare dismiss me, or I will make you pay!"

"I wouldn't dream of it, my Lord. You know we always favoured you, so beautiful, even more beautiful than Kanaloa. Don't tell him we said so."

"Stop playing games with me. I demand you stop all access to my dreams immediately!"

"Done."

"If I hear of it again, we'll meet face to face."

"I would enjoy that."

"No. You wouldn't," I snapped.

Felix blinked, looked at me. He was back. "Did I say something?"

"Yes, and none of it was good. I don't want you talking to what's his name anymore."

"But he... Okay." He hung his head. "Fine. But..." He trailed off.

"Yes?" I lifted an eyebrow.

"You must promise to leave that human boy alone."

"He's not a boy, and I promise not to see him again. It's over." As I said it, I felt the pain, more severe than the pain of any sunlight on my face. "Now" — I cleared my throat and pointed at the board, desperate for a change of topic — "will you make your move already?"

Felix glanced at me, and nodded. "You're right, Kane. It's time for the king to make a move," and holding my gaze, he moved the king pawn two spaces forward.

Chapter Three

I felt a strangeness I couldn't explain as the weeks went by. I felt almost as if I were in a movie, or perhaps on a stage, and the world was watching me. Unlike some of my friends, I'd never harboured a fantasy or even a true desire to be an actor, but I'd suddenly found myself in the midst of this strange universe where around me, behind me, closing in on my every move, were shadowy images, whispering voices.

I began to see things. Ghostly things. I saw things nobody else could see, at least they said they couldn't. One evening just after dusk, Evelin and I sat out in the backyard sharing a bottle of Volcano Winery's signature red wine. The Volcano Red, which retailed for around twenty dollars a bottle, had been the gift of a grateful local businessman whom I had helped transport to Honolulu for emergency heart surgery.

We'd even opened her new, stemless glasses that naturally aerated wine the moment the liquid hit the insides. We sipped, cradling the bowls in our warm hands.

"No wonder they call this Pele's Delight," Evelin said. "I had no idea we actually had some decent vineyards here in the islands."

"Neither did I. And you're right. This is really good."

"Did you ever find that restaurant Malakai took you to?" she asked. "Because I've asked around and nobody's heard of it."

"Nope. I never did." It hurt to think about it actually. I missed the man so much.

We savoured each drop of the blend of grapes and the rare jaboticaba berry. I'd never heard of this particular berry until Evelin and I researched the wine's history. Lately I'd been drawn more and more to wine, particularly red. I liked sashimi, I liked steak tartare. I sipped my wine and held it in my mouth a moment, able to smell lava, berries, smoke and deep red earth before I swallowed.

I heard a sound and looked to my left. I quite clearly saw a woman, Asian by the looks of things, with a very small child. They stood, very still, almost in awe, watching Evelin and me.

"Hi," I said, straightening up on my chaise.

"Who are you talking to?" Evelin looked wide-eyed as she held up the bottle in her hand and refilled her glass.

"Them." I pointed to the woman and child. "We don't bite," I announced to the pair. They didn't respond but they didn't flee either. "I think we have some juice for your boy and there's a little wine left." I glanced at the bottle.

"Who are you talking to?" Evelin said again.

I looked at her. "Don't you see them?"

"See who?" She craned forward, almost dropping the bottle. She squinted into the encroaching darkness.

"I don't see anybody." She sounded more frustrated than anything else. "What do they look like?"

The woman had placed a protective arm around her son and they backed away a little towards the tropical foliage lining the back fence. The child kept his grave stare on my face, his mother's hand resting on his shoulder.

"A beautiful woman and a little boy." My throat went dry. "You don't see them, do you." It was a statement more than a question.

"No, sweetheart, I don't." She glanced at me. "What are they doing now?"

I didn't respond right away because I'd just realised the woman's hand had no fingers. She also seemed scantily clad. They were frightened. They seemed to know that I meant them no harm, but I heard a crack of thunder and the woman reacted. The little boy began to wail. It was a horrible, merciless sound.

"Tell me you can't hear that." I turned to Evelin who was staring at me in an odd way.

"Hear what?" she asked.

"The kid screaming. The crack of thunder."

I smelt smoke now. Volcano smoke, only it wasn't a fresh eruption. I heard chanting, the disturbing yet hypnotic chant of Night Marchers. I could feel them marching. They beat drum gourds in rhythm. Their pounding feet and smashing drums were so loud and so deep they rattled my teeth.

They were coming for the woman and child.

She heard them too and grabbed her son. She said something I didn't understand and vanished. She simply disappeared.

And so too, did the chant of the Night Marchers.

Wow. I'd either had too much of Pele's Delight or I'd tapped into some parallel universe.

"What do they look like?" Evelin suddenly asked.

"They're gone."

Out of the corner of my eye, I caught Evelin's nod. "I figured. You seem more relaxed now. Tell me, are they local?"

I hesitated. The word *local* was a weighted one in the islands. So many ethnicities had mingled here for generations. There were some islanders though who yearned for a return to native rule and considered those who didn't have Hawaiian blood to be *local*. But not Hawaiian. The criteria had become more strident the last couple of years. Some people predicted a violent war was brewing, but I doubted that. Even when our monarchy had been overthrown by the Americans and our queen imprisoned, there'd been no war. Only supreme grief.

To me, however, anyone whose family had lived here for some time and gave to the land and loved it was local. And Hawaiian.

"They're not native," I said. I had begun to worry about the mother and child. They had displeased some deity, I was certain. The Big Island was a haven for restless souls. I saw them often. I had no idea why but I had begun to suspect I must have almost died when I was in the hospital and I'd traversed the line between the seen and unseen worlds.

I didn't discuss this issue much since there was nobody I could talk to about it who wouldn't think I was nuts. All day and night my mind chanted one name. *Malakai. Malakai. Malakai.* But the man had vanished. A different sort of ghost. He was real. I knew that but exactly what he was, I had no idea. I wondered if Malakai was some kind of fugitive from justice. He came and went, his imprint left a little louder and deeper on my soul each time, but there was no telling when he'd materialise.

Or when he would leave again...

Sometimes I took walks to the spot on the highway where I'd first seen my lover. I would walk to the mountain top where Malakai's house had stood. And I felt crazy, yes, plum crazy, Pele's Delight rare berry crazy that I thought the things I did, but I felt certain, absolutely positive that Malakai's house was there. It was just...hidden. I'd never mentioned this to anyone, but I felt the house was somehow veiled. Secretly hidden from view but there, right *there*, just out of reach. I sometimes went when I couldn't sleep, which was a lot lately. I sensed Malakai there, needing my presence.

At times it seemed Malakai was a dream, but I knew the man was real. He'd come to me in the hospital and saved my life. Was he a guardian angel? A deep, dark, secret biting angel? Because I could swear I had dreams of the main biting me but not to kill me. I had weird, erotic dreams where I came over and over again, the man's teeth imbedded in my throat and his cock planted deep inside my ass.

I trembled a moment thinking about our late-night encounters that seemed to come in my sleep, but I knew they were real. I had too much evidence they were real...I just couldn't explain them. Not to myself. Not to anyone.

"Like I said, they're not native, but they are local." I could still sense their terror, but they were beyond my reach, my natural inclination to help. A breeze crossed my face, like ghostly fingertips stroking my very soul, letting me know something...*somebody* was close. Not Malakai. No. My internal temperature always rose when I sensed Malakai's nearness. I had never been so aware of another man before.

It was as if Malakai had awoken me from a very long sleep. I both recognised the spirituality in all things and the unique divinity of even a simple leaf. Sometimes it frightened me, such as now, with the mother and son. I knew they were ghosts, their spirits restless...lost. But I had no idea how to help them. I wondered why they had come into the garden. I held my glass out for more wine, aware of Evelin's slight hesitance to pour me some.

She filled my glass halfway. When had it become fashionable to do this? It always made me feel restaurants and friends were afraid to fill glasses in case they ran out of wine.

"Are you hungry?" I asked, sipping at mine again.

I could tell this surprised her. "You rarely eat anymore, I'm glad you're at least thinking about food, and yes, I am. I don't feel like cooking, though."

"I thought maybe we could have dinner at the Volcano House. My treat."

She brightened noticeably at the suggestion. "I'd love it. I'm surprised though. Most people only like to go during the day when they can see the view. As you know, you can't see the volcano from the windows there at night."

Ah...that's where she's wrong. I can see it. I see everything at night. I see things nobody else does. Not that I can tell her that.

I didn't know whether my new sensory perception was a good thing or not. At times I felt isolated, even more alone than ever. I withdrew into myself frequently, especially when I saw the dead and couldn't tell them apart from the living. I'd seen a ghost once when I was with Jon and it had totally freaked him out.

"You know you're different since you came back from the hospital," Evelin remarked.

"So I keep hearing. How do I…? In what way do I seem different to you?"

Jon said I was spooky. He told our boss Kimo I creeped him out. Does everyone feel that way? I kept my gaze on the glass in my hand. It still seemed weird to be holding a glass with no stem. Something was missing. Like me. Something fundamental had gone even though I had so much more now.

Malakai…

His name was a whisper on the wind.

I felt the ghostly, chilled fingertips across my cheek and jumped. Maybe it *was* Malakai. Sometimes I felt the man close, caught my shadow, my scent.

"You seem more grounded and yet more open somehow."

I delighted in her statement. She seemed relieved that I wasn't offended, but how could I be? She was right. I'd been so…fixed…before I became sick. Now I felt all those around me were the ones who saw only black and white, who had a hard time accepting what had happened to me, my near-fatal illness.

A few people even questioned whether I was completely well. Even Jon. Oh, we were still flight partners, but ever since I had witnessed a traffic accident in Jon's company and the accident had turned out to be a ghostly occurrence, my friend's confidence in me had shattered.

I had even been forced to submit to a urine test for drugs. Drugs! I took the test and even offered up blood work, though Kimo had insisted urinalysis was adequate. The test had shown a high level of blood glucose but absolutely no drugs in my system. My doctors back in Honolulu had told Kimo that the strong medicines I'd taken, especially the mixture of antibiotics, could have caused the elevated sugar levels. They had been appalled that I had even come under scrutiny.

"He's lucky to be alive," they'd told Kimo who had cowered under their criticism. "How dare you accuse him when he's done nothing but fight to live?"

And since I had been more dedicated than ever to my work, the ugly incident over the ghostly car wreck remained unspoken between me and Jon. The chasm between us might have been growing wider and wider in our personal lives, but professionally we were still a good team. Or, at least I liked to think so.

Tonight was my night off and I longed to be close to the volcano, to see it in all its glory.

"You sure you really want to go out for dinner?" Evelin seemed so thrilled. I knew that lately I had gone from enjoying my freedom from the hospital to wanting to be still and quiet, absorbing everything that presented itself to me.

I usually declined her invitations, not because I didn't enjoy her company but because for some odd reason I felt she somehow knew what was going on with me. I sensed her watching and almost reading me. Her intuition, her knowledge of the infinite had amused and somewhat irritated me when I'd first moved in.

Woo-woo, and airy-fairy some people called her. A hippie. A throwback. A sixties reject. Overgrown flower child. But I knew she was so much more. Evelin was deeply connected and concerned about the land and even more so about the ancestors. She believed in all the ancient deities, knew them as one would know a distant relative. She talked of Ku, Kane, Kanaloa, Pele, Hina…as the guardians of the islands as they were, but also as if they were living people.

Lately I was beginning to wonder if she knew more than she let on, that she…suspected things, especially about Malakai. She was the only person I knew that had actually met him and on a couple of occasions she'd remarked on running into him. One time she'd told me Malakai had come to the house looking for me.

"Really?" I'd asked. "What did he say?"

"It's the strangest thing," she'd said. "He didn't speak to me. I told him you were at work and he nodded. Next thing I knew, he was hugging me."

I had never been so jealous in my whole life.

"And then, I know this sounds bizarre, but he kissed me. My neck, I mean. I must have fainted or something because I woke up in bed and my neck stung a little. I'm wondering if I was stung by a bee and he took the stinger out with his teeth. I'm highly allergic to bees, you know." She'd fallen silent for a moment then told me she was almost certain Malakai had saved her life because she'd felt near death. Her life had flashed before her eyes and everything.

We lay back once again in companionable silence enjoying the wine. I loved the earthy smell of it, combined with the pleasant smoke of somebody's backyard barbecue.

"Sausages," I proclaimed. I could almost hear them sizzling. I experienced a moment of relief when she nodded and sniffed appreciatively. The barbecue was real. I hadn't totally lost my last marble.

We took the rest of the wine and our empty glasses back inside, the heat of the day still evident in the kitchen. It was the last room to heat up each day, but it held its warmth even as the temperature plummeted overnight.

"You want to drive or should I?" she asked, corking what was left of the volcanic wine.

I caught a shimmery movement out of the corner of my eye. A gravitational pull. *Holy cow*. Malakai. I looked again. Nothing. I fought all my instincts to rush to my room and get naked for the seductions that only happened late at night alone in my bed. No more dates. No more cell phone messages, texts.

No more dates.

That part I couldn't sidestep.

Malakai didn't want to be with me. He wanted to fuck me. He was an elegant booty call. I couldn't keep living like this, poised between sleeplessness and fate. I wanted a man. A partner. A lover. A real one. I wanted to be with somebody who felt shipwrecked without me. Was I asking too much? Everybody else I knew had lovers. Even Jon. I didn't necessarily think Jon had the perfect match but it hurt me often, knowing that as I struggled to both grasp and release the dream of Malakai, Jon was allowed to screw up his life with a real asshole.

And there lay the key issue. Sometimes I could be logical about my feelings for Malakai and the strange relationship we had. Other times I experienced such strong…visions, clear images that Malakai wanted to be with me but *couldn't*.

Maybe now I was a little liquored up I sensed Malakai's strong desire for me but some unknown barrier remained between us. I couldn't let go of him because I loved him. And besides, Malakai wouldn't let go of *me*. It had been six days since he'd apparently come to the house and run into Evelin.

Since then, neither of us had glimpsed him. I was glad I had Evelin to talk about Malakai with. I knew I wasn't crazy when she talked about him. I blew out a breath.

"You drive. I think I might have had a touch more wine than you."

She smiled. "I drank more than you did but really, we had a couple of glasses each and it's not that far. Should I change?"

Oh, brother. I knew she wanted to, but for cripes' sake, it was just me and her and it wasn't a date. But she seemed oddly lonely too these days so I let her go. I contemplated going to my room while I waited, but she checked her watch.

"I'm just going to grab my pea coat," she said. "It gets so cold up there. Think we need to book?"

No. "I'll call, just in case."

That made her happy. When I called the Volcano House I was surprised to find they had one spot left open at eight o'clock. I shouldn't have been so shocked. The newly remodelled restaurant and cabin-style hotel was still the only game in town for front row seats to nature's handiwork.

"We're slammed," the owner told me, hardly able to keep the glee from his voice. "Please don't be late or we will reassign your table."

"We'll be there." I should have guessed that since Kilauea's eruption, tourism had increased on the island. Tourists were so weird. They all *wanted* to rent the lava-damaged vehicles and purchase lava-ruined flowers. They would post photos on Facebook. *Look what Madame Pele did to our car! We were so close to the eruption!*

People were so anxious for an authentic experience they were willing to lie about it...

Evelin emerged from her bedroom in a new shirt, her hair brushed and her coat over her arm. The truth was the temperatures could get below zero high up on the volcanic slope, even though the crater itself still smouldered. Kilauea always smouldered and besides, the actual fiery path of her recent activity was a couple of miles deep into the crater's trail.

"We've got thirty minutes to get there," I told her. I tried not to be disappointed that Malakai hadn't tried to seduce me with his phantasmagoric presence in the few minutes Evelin had gone.

Maybe we're both dreaming.

Maybe we're both nuts...

Evelin took time constraints as a direct challenge and as we bustled out of the house I couldn't help but notice her paintings in the living room. The explosive volcano. Pele. Malakai.

Malakai was even more powerful a presence than the great volcano goddess.

Did Evelin see him as some kind of a god?

In the realm of deities, Pele was a profound presence but Kane and Kanaloa were the most revered and feared. Pele had loyal devotees and certainly had proven herself capable of great destruction but in the painting I stopped to stare at now, Malakai took the form of an ancient deity challenging her to stop. The great goddess was on the ground kneeling, looking up at him as if begging him for mercy.

I couldn't believe this particular imagery. I couldn't imagine Pele kneeling before any man...couldn't even begin to process the idea she would be afraid of any god or man.

Something in the representation of Malakai, however, made me shake my head in wonderment. Evelin too, could feel his power, his secret depths.

His pain…

Yes. It was there in his eyes. She'd captured it. His loneliness.

He was a thousand years old. Or more.

Why me? I asked myself then chided the foolish notion that after centuries of being alone, impervious to human pleasures and peccadilloes he'd walked out of the fiery cone of Kilauea and chosen me as a lover.

But that was exactly what had happened. He'd walked out of the smoking, volcanic rainforest and…claimed me.

Evelin tugged my sleeve. "You picked a fine time to start appreciating my art," she joked.

"I always appreciate your art," I protested. "That painting is amazing."

She dragged me out of the door. Yes, Evelin had seen something in Malakai that I had, too. Someday I had to get her good and snockered and ask her what was what.

"You captured him well," I said. She fired up the SUV she'd bought from a Japanese couple who'd sold up all their homes in Tokyo and the mainland and moved to the Big Island. They'd opened a coffee shop. They'd returned to their point of origin like most foreigners within twelve months.

"This island is too big," the wife had told me and Evelin when I'd gone with her to test drive the almost new vehicle. "I miss being cramped. I miss noise."

Since my near-death experience I craved space and quiet. I couldn't relate at all. I'd approved Evelin's purchase however. I would have barked at her had she been stupid enough to ship a vehicle like this to the island as the Japanese couple had. New vehicles depreciated the second they touched Hawaiian land due to sand and salt corrosion and the high rate of car vandalism.

For Evelin it meant a vehicle with no problems, not counting the high insurance rate she now lived with and it meant some extra little luxuries such as seat warmers. I cranked up the heat as she hurtled up the mountainous Crater Rim Drive.

For nearly three years the Volcano House restaurant had been closed and had slowly reopened its sandwich bar and gift shop, then its hotel rooms, and finally the restaurant itself. It had been a spectacular remodel and I had deep fantasies of spending a night in one of the cabin rooms with Malakai making crazy love as we looked out over the volcano.

In the meantime, I would have to settle for one of the restaurant's signature 'ohelo berry shakes. Thick and vibrant red, the shakes were made of the berry sacred to Pele. A cousin of the cranberry, 'ohelo were very bitter but very tasty when added to sugar and milk. The restaurant prided itself on following the Hawaiian tradition of asking the goddess for permission to pick her berries and throw a few into the crater before picking some for its own use.

Failure to do so brought rain and her legendary flashes of temper.

We arrived at the restaurant with mere seconds to spare. The concept of valet parking had mercifully not reached Volcano House yet but I thought I spotted a man in uniform pacing outside the front. I blinked and looked again. Nothing.

As we walked inside, I could smell the satisfying odour of sulphuric gases. The volcano still ruled. I could see the molten lava peeking beneath the crater's rim glowing through the big picture window. I almost crowed with delight.

It hadn't been an accident that I could see so far in the distance now. The planets and constellations were a gauzy lightshow for me. I really could see things others couldn't. I really could!

I didn't know what to do with my new abilities and wondered why they'd been given to me. The truth was I'd gone on a partying binge when I first came out of the hospital because I thought I was going crazy.

Now I felt I was being groomed...almost. I was being prepared for something...but what? Even as I took Evelin's coat and handed it to the waiter, I felt a tingling sense of expectation as I watched the man hang it up with the others. I could tell things about the fibres of clothing. Could sense their tight or even loose weave. I shook my head at myself, something I did a lot these days.

There was beauty and pain, even in a seemingly inanimate object. I closed my ears to the apparent screaming of a lamb's wool sweater hanging beside the coat. I knew somehow that the lamb had sensed an older sheep's wool in the coat.

I could hear it baa-ing.

Mama.

I almost ran from the restaurant. When I heard these voices they still freaked me out. I distracted myself by peering out at the packed tables.

"Jepoi."

I started. Looking around, I couldn't see who the voice belonged to. The waiter had grabbed a couple of menus and began to show us to our table. I scanned the diners.

"I'm here. Heh, heh, heh. Can't you see me?"

It was a voice I didn't recognise.

My God. There was Jon with a guy I had never seen before. He appeared to be middle-aged, brown hair slicked back. There was something about him that I didn't trust...or like. I tried to disabuse myself of this notion but as we stopped and greeted them, Jon seemed very uncomfortable as he introduced us to his dining companion.

"This is Starzs," he said. "We met in the oddest way."

Starzs leaned across the table and covered Jon's hand with his own. Then he stood and shook my hand. He was wearing a robe, as if he were some kind of Roman emperor. It was a freaky getup in a part of the islands that had just about seen it all.

"A pleasure, Jepoi." He also added, "Evelin," but his gaze never left my face. And I knew now the man had somehow talked to me in my mind. My skin prickled and I put my hand at the small of Evelin's back to lead her away.

"What a weirdo," Evelin whispered as we reached our table. We ordered the house shakes and the waiter brought them to us a few minutes later.

"I'll be back in a moment to take your food orders," the waiter said.

"Take your time." I wasn't sure I could eat. I'd order another shake. Maybe something light. Evelin was already considering whether to choose steak or chicken as we raised our glasses in a toast. I suddenly became aware of a strong presence.

I almost swooned when I glanced into the window that overlooked the crater and saw Malakai's reflection beside our table. I turned and looked but Malakai wasn't there. Some instinct told me we had to get out, had to leave *now*. I was startled to see Jon and Starzs getting up to leave.

"We have to go," I said.

"Leave? But we just got here." Evelin looked devastated.

"Do you trust me?" I asked Evelin. I pulled out my wallet, peeled off a twenty dollar bill and left it on the table.

"Yes," she said simply.

We got up to leave, maybe half a minute behind Jon and his friend Starzs.

"Can you tell me what's going on?" Evelin asked as she lifted her coat from its hook on the rack.

"I don't know what's going on, only that we have to hurry."

By the time we got outside and reached the car, Jon and his companion had gone. Evelin hurried down the crater road, the glow of the other car's tail lights within view.

"Are we following them?" she asked.

"Yes." I could see by the turned heads and the occasional flashes of light that Jon and Starzs were arguing.

"What's going on between them?" Evelin asked. Obviously she could tell something was wrong, too.

"I don't know." I was worried now. What if the immense warning I'd received was a mind trick?

Evelin followed a pace or two behind them as we neared civilisation again. Once they reached a crossroads, she glanced at me.

"They just turned onto Highway thirty-one. Should I follow?"

"Yes." I was stunned to see a car running a red light right in front of them and hitting a motorcycle as the rider was making a left turn. The crashing sound of metal upon metal sickened me. I gripped the door handle as the motor cyclist rose from the bike and bounced off the roof of the vehicle that hit him then landed on the ground.

For one split-second I didn't react. After my last ghastly episode with Jon, I feared I was seeing ghosts but I knew it was real. I jumped out of the vehicle and ran to the prone cyclist.

"Call 911!" I screamed at Evelin.

"Got it!" she called back.

Kneeling beside the man, I searched for a pulse and got one. A faint one.

"Let him go."

I knew the voice now. It was that Starzs guy. But where the hell was he? I looked around in the thick gloom, the sparse street lights giving me little to work with. With my new heightened senses I probably could have seen Starzs but I needed to focus on the injured man at my side.

"911 operator wants to talk to you." Evelin brought me her cell phone. I talked to the operator who promised me an ambulance was on its way.

"I'm a flight nurse for—"

"I know who you are. Do you think the patient requires evac?"

"Yes. I think he has a broken neck." From the awkward angle of his neck, I was certain of it.

The man remained unconscious as I tried to make him more comfortable before the paramedics arrived without dislodging his broken neck.

"I'll have Hawaii Air Patrol waiting at Hilo Airport," she said. "Pulse rate?"

As I followed up with manual checks on his heartbeat, the man began to convulse.

"He's having a grand mal seizure," I said. As the man's body went into the clonic phase of a seizure, contracting and spasming, I had no idea if he experienced seizures normally or if these were a result of severe head injury. I stayed right with the man, Evelin suddenly kneeling beside me.

She kept her hands on the man's trembling body, saying over and over again, "*Uhane nui.*" It was a Hawaiian blessing meaning, *I am spirit greatness.* She was trying to infuse positive thought into the man's aura. The thrashing stopped after two minutes and we relaxed. A wail of sirens.

"*Let him go. He belongs to the other side.*"

"No!" I shouted, looking up to see Starzs standing across the road watching me.

I became aware of a distinct presence beside me.

Malakai.

A war of silent words went on between the two men. The sirens grew louder, closer. The man on the ground began convulsing again, his strongest contractions happening as the paramedics jumped from the vehicle.

My cell phone rang and Starzs turned and walked away from us.

"What an asshole," Evelin said. She turned back to our patient and kept whispering soothing words to him. I recognised the man as the paramedics turned him over carefully with my help and with Malakai's. They placed the patient's head in portable traction equipment that would keep his neck stable. The man's eyes fluttered open.

"My neck hurts," he whimpered.

"How −?" Evelin gasped when she recognised the patient. It was Jon.

Jon…it still didn't make sense. How the hell had he gone from being in a car with Starzs to being on a motorbike coming from a different direction?

Malakai vanished. I sensed it rather than saw him leave.

"What the hell…" Evelin looked stunned as Jon moaned on the ground. Every single movement had him crying out in pain. She gazed up at me totally perplexed and frightened. I knew I hadn't imagined the encounter in the restaurant or the urge to follow Jon home.

"I'll go with him," I told her as the paramedics loaded Jon up into the ambulance. She nodded and hugged me. She cried as I left, but I was beyond grief or even surprise anymore, as Jon and I made the trip to the airport.

I knew he would survive, that he would make it. Malakai had made sure. What bargain had he made with the devil? Or had he thwarted a god?

The heavens cracked open, thunder and lightning piercing the night as we made the journey to the tarmac in record time.

Miffy Hutchence, a new arrival from the mainland, joined me on the plane and it didn't surprise me when nature's sky dance stopped as we prepped for departure.

Our pilot was Alex and he gave me a thumbs-up. I trusted and liked Miffy, a middle-aged woman who'd left an abusive girlfriend to begin her life anew on the Big Island.

I accompanied Jon, taking care of him all the way on the one hour flight to Honolulu. Lightning lit the night sky as we landed. Our boss Kimo called our cell phones and told me, Miffy, and Alex that the weather was too precarious to fly back tonight. He'd organised rooms at a standard Hawaiian hotel where he got great rates. The Queen Kapiolani. Poised on the edge of Waikiki overlooking the gay end of the island of

Oahu. I loved the dense night sky and the view of Diamond Head in front of my windows.

As I locked my door and opened the windows to look outside, I sensed a presence and turned.

When I saw Malakai gliding towards me, I surrendered myself to him completely. But just like that, he vanished.

For a moment I felt my soul had been ripped in two, except it wasn't my soul at stake. But his. I felt his screaming. I felt his pain.

"Oh God, Malakai," I whispered into the silent room. "What have you done?"

Chapter Four

"You will cause another volcano to erupt, Kane, if you don't calm down." The voices all blended into one, surrounding me as if attempting to stay my fury. I was standing upright now, the pain having forced me to my knees initially. Now, all that suffering had blossomed into full-blown rage.

If it is any solace, Kane, we suffer with you. We had no choice. You have been warned not to interfere.

"You are all his slaves now," I shot back. "There is no longer any independent justice, no objectivity. You are blind to what is going on beneath your very noses! Starzs is not a soul taker, he is a dream merchant. So, ask yourselves what he was doing walking around in full view of mortals and stealing a soul? May I remind you, it was the soul of Jepoi's friend!"

I waited for them to explain that away. Finally, the voice returned from somewhere in the murky skies around me. It sounded faint, less sure. "If you are making an accusation before this council, then please be clear! And make sure you have proof to back up your claim."

"You know full well what I'm saying. Starzs was not acting alone. He does not have that power. Only Kanaloa has that kind of power and he would never lower himself to..." I stopped. "He gave *him* the power, either that, or he stole it."

We know not of whom you speak, Kane.

"Yes, you do," I sneered. "This is all about vengeance. How did he get it? Kanaloa would never just hand it over so, that's it, he stole it and he enlisted Starzs to help him."

There was no response. I didn't expect one. I pointed at the clouds. "You can punish me all you want, try and rip out my heart again, but you can't do it. You'll never do it."

I turned to go.

"Kane!"

I turned to see Brodaine, one of the principal members standing in front of me. His long white hair almost hit the floor. It was rare they'd actually physically manifest. I bowed slightly, but my respect for the council was waning.

My eyes widened suddenly as Brodaine bowed to me. "I have such faith that you will be restored to your former place. The universe is not in balance and we are afraid that darkness will reign forever unless you are restored. You must remember who you are, and work to challenge him. The curse can be broken, Kane."

"I haven't forgotten who I am." I stiffened.

"Then stay away from that mortal."

"I have done the best I can in that respect. I feel he is in danger. I cannot leave him out there defenceless. The attack on Jon was a warning. He wants Jepoi. I can't allow an innocent to be hurt because I chose to make love to him."

"You must settle this between you, you and —"

I put up my hand. "Don't speak his name in my presence ever." I paused. "If he is indeed doing this without Kanaloa's knowledge then perhaps someone should let him know?" I raised an eyebrow in his direction.

"It is not our place to do that. We are an impartial body and not permitted to interfere."

"I'm not sure about your impartiality."

He bowed again. "It is true, but our hearts are with you, Kane. Please, believe this."

"Then I guess it will be up to me then."

"You must be careful. He has devices, ways to make your existence even more miserable. You have to have a plan. You are all immortals. It's not like you can kill him. And we don't want that. We need you both."

"Thanks for the advice and the...punishment." I walked away through the swirl of mist and fog only to find Felix waiting in the clearing. When he saw me, he flew up in the air after me. I grabbed him and let him ride on my shoulders.

"Are you all right?" He appeared to shudder. "I heard your agony."

"I'm fine. More pain on a different day. No surprise." We were inside the sanctuary of the house. I put Felix down and paced. Felix watched me silently, biting his fingernails. "Did you know?" I asked him.

He shook his head. "I would have told you, you know that."

"But you have pity for that...prick."

"I only feel his broken heart, his regret. You know how I internalise things. I remember a time when you were happy...together."

"This is not about regret, it's about vengeance. And I don't care to go down memory lane. He has gone behind my back and Kanaloa's too. He tried to kill Jepoi's friend, Jon. Worse, he has enlisted that sleazy dream merchant to help him do it!"

"It's a cry for help."

I shot him a dirty look. "Take me to Starzs."

"Now?" Felix slid back into the corner. "He won't like that."

"Yes. Now. And I like it even less."

He sighed.

"You know where to find him and I need to stop this."

"You only want to protect that mortal."

"My reasons are my own. Just do as I ask."

"I have to see if he's available." Felix looked hesitant. "He's a busy guy."

"Busy or not, he's about to have company."

"Kane…now…hold your temper, okay? Don't cause another volcano to—"

"Felix"—I walked over and looked down into his eyes—"let's go."

He nodded, reached up and took my hand. A few minutes later, we were in the middle of Starzs' club. Several misty figures floated around. Some bizarre music was being played by robotic looking rockers and the bartender at the end of the room poured endless fizzy beverages with colourful little umbrellas planted in fruit.

Starzs sat on a velvet chair up on a pedestal as if on centre stage. Some man in an executive suit was on his knees in front of him pleading for something. Starzs' focus was suddenly centred on me. He couldn't seem to stop smiling as I approached. "Take this fool away," he muttered, indicating the businessman to a huge guy with a shiny stick in his hand.

"Malakai!" He clapped his hands together as if he'd just had the most delightful experience. "How nice of you to pay me a visit. Come closer so that I may inhale your presence."

Starzs was a tall, gaunt figure who was fond of God-like robes, often trimmed in gold. He wasn't at all attractive, but some found him charismatic. His slick head was adorned with sparkles and what looked like a holly wreath or it might have been leaves.

"Taking yourself for emperor, now?" I asked him.

"Nasty boy, but then you always did have some wit even back when Kane ruled. And I did say I was pleased to receive you. Don't make me out a liar. So, to what do I owe the honour?" He didn't even acknowledge Felix who hid behind me.

"What business have you with Kanaloa's paramour?"

He laughed, his eyes sparkling. "My, you are some beauty. I think the curse enhances it."

"Answer my question!"

He laughed again.

My patience was wearing thin. "Did I say something amusing?" I demanded.

"You still can't bring yourself to say his name, can you?"

I decided not to answer.

"Well"—he shrugged, arranging his long white robe—"when someone is in need...I lend him a hand, that's all, just being neighbourly."

"Neighbourly? You stole one of Kanaloa's powers. Do you know what he'll do to you if he finds out?"

Starzs noticeably stiffened. "I did one little favour! And I didn't steal anything."

"You helped *him* to steal it. You are as guilty as he. And you tried to take a mortal's soul. It wasn't his time. You had no business doing that and indeed, no valid reason. You distracted Kanaloa with a dream and then let his little slut steal that power."

"If you came here looking for the power, I don't have it," he grunted.

I climbed the steps to his self-made throne. The big man with the stick took a few steps towards me. I turned, put up my hand as I took Starzs around the neck with the other hand. "Come any farther," I said over my shoulder, "and your master will be in pieces."

"He means it," Starzs croaked, gasping for breath. "Stop, Murden."

I looked down into his face. "Now, answer my question. Does that snake still have the power to take human souls, or not?"

Starzs nodded frantically.

"Now, you're going to tell me what his next move is going to be, or I'm going to contact a former friend of mine, and tell him just what you've been up to. Is that clear?"

I released him.

He rubbed his throat. No one in the club batted an eye. I suspected they were all dreaming. I pulled Starzs to his feet. "Now, let's go someplace quiet where we can talk. And if you say his name once, I'll drink you dry. Is that clear?"

"Crystal." He flashed some white teeth at me.

"Good."

A few minutes later I was in his sitting room. He floated around like a social butterfly, offering me all kinds of things. "Sit!" I told him.

"So demanding and dominating, ooh." He chuckled. "I do want you to reconsider appearing in my dreams.

I'll have the contracts drawn up. Twenty per cent, how does that sound or—?"

I'd had enough. "It's Jepoi, isn't it?" I demanded. "He plans to take his soul next."

"Brains and beauty," he murmured.

"Why are you getting involved in this?"

"Business isn't what it used to be. I've got the same actors over and over in the bloody dreams. We've run out of beauties. And the economy is not quite as—"

I sighed. "What's in it for you?"

"He's promised to send business my way."

"How, by manipulating mortals to increase their dream quotas?"

"I'm not sure but—"

"How and where?"

"What?"

"How and where is he going to attack Jepoi?"

"Ah…I really don't have the…"

I stood, making my intention clear. "I will rip you apart."

Something in my face made him sing a different tune. "Tomorrow night. I need to plant a dream in Jepoi's mind that will prompt him to get up out of his sleep and go to the beach. He plans to lead him into the water to drown."

I closed my eyes. "Damn. Okay. You're to say nothing, you understand me? Go ahead as planned. I will be there waiting."

"You'll be there anyway. The figure calling to him…is you. That mortal is really hung up."

"What a bastard Kanaloa is."

"Revenge sucks big time."

I pointed at him. "Yes, it does and you're about to experience it first-hand if you alert him. I will carry through with my threat and let Kanaloa know what you've been up to with his lover."

Fear crossed the dream merchant's face. "All right, all right. Don't fret. I'll do it."

I walked to the exit.

He followed. "So," he said, as I headed to the door, "how about that offer to star in my dreams? You'll be a celebrity. A former god cursed to be a demon blood drinker, hot, hot and…oh…yeah…you know? I'll be rich."

I walked out and let the door slam behind me. That was my answer.

Felix was sniggering.

I glanced up at him. "What's with you?"

"I like it so much when you're rude. It suits you."

I glared at him. "Don't think you're off the hook for your role in all this."

His expression changed to that pout of his. "Ohhhh," he moaned. "I didn't say I liked it that much when you get this way."

The rest of the way back to the house, Felix pleaded his case, but I didn't hear most of what he said. I was focused on Jepoi, and worried that harm would come to him.

I lay down on the bed upon my return and closed my eyes. I remembered touching him, fucking him, and it soothed me. What amazed me was as hard as I tried to banish thoughts of me, memories of my visits, even my house, he retained them.

It scared me to think that our connection was so strong I couldn't break those invisible bonds between us. I was grateful now because I needed them.

I won't let anything happen to you.

He had some of my blood. It would give resistance, extra sensory capacity. Maybe that was why, try as I did, he remembered things. For a moment, I felt his loneliness and suffering, the ache, not just for me, but for some understanding. Jepoi had no idea what was happening to him. Our bond, whatever I sent to his dreams, would help, but he was no match for...

I sighed. I'd have to say his damn name eventually. I'd survived in denial. If I didn't speak his name, he no longer existed to me. But he did exist. It was just a game I was playing. And he was back, trying to punish me for finding some physical pleasure in another. *I'm not yours anymore.*

When I'd said those words so long ago, they'd burned like fire. Now, they merely echoed in the room without meaning. Kanaloa had ensured I'd be alone by cursing me. There wasn't much for either of us to worry about. I couldn't actually be with Jepoi all the time. We stole our moments. So. Why take his soul?

Because you desire him.

Those words were whispered around me. I wasn't sure if I'd said them myself or if someone else had. Didn't matter. I let my eyes close and fell asleep.

Images of volcanoes erupting, people scattering, the skies opening up, rain and thunder...the balance would forever be affected after that dark night. The earth changed, famine, war, intolerance and hatred...and here I was, part of the nightmare.

I reached out and touched Jepoi in his sleep. "Hold me," I said softly. "I need your body, your blood, but I won't take your soul. That's your most intimate possession."

When I opened my eyes, Felix was sitting on my chest, staring at me. "Are you angry?"

"Get off me," I told him.

He snuggled down beside me. "I love you. I'd do nothing to hurt you, but I worry. You are so reckless, Malakai. You should have been the god of chaos."

"And you" —I touched his nose— "should mind your own business."

He smiled. "You love me still."

"Yes," I said. "Just don't play games. They get away from you."

"Okay. Where you going?" he asked as I got out of bed.

"You know where. I need to speak to him, warn him."

"Is it the last time?" He followed me around the room, hopping on one arm.

"It will be if he is no longer in danger."

"Are you planning on making love to him again?"

I left the room and he hobbled after me.

"Kane?"

"No, I'm not planning on it." I smiled. "But I can't guarantee I won't."

"You'll pee off the council again."

"Oh, really?" I grinned. "Good a reason as any for doing it then."

"That's bad." He chuckled.

"Stay here, and don't get into any trouble," I warned.

He nodded.

I leant down and kissed his head and he smiled.

Making it to Oahu took some ingenuity. I hadn't travelled interisland on my own steam for some time. Now I'd gone twice in a few months, first to save Jepoi and now I was heading back again.

Rain poured as I landed in the driveway of the Queen Kapiolani Hotel. The island was already being pummelled by a bad storm yet, it was late and the hotel was quiet tonight. The weather had been quite unpredictable, which had cut down on tourists. I suspected someone I wasn't about to name had something to do with this tumultuous weather.

I walked the lobby for a moment and glanced up. I knew Jepoi was on the third floor of the hotel. I would have preferred to talk to him outside, but there was no time to waste. It was late and soon he would go to bed.

I glided by the desk clerk and took the elevator to the third floor. Before I got to the door, I saw it was ajar. I saw Jepoi staring out of the sliding glass doors at the now raging storm. Lightning and thunder peppered the sky. He turned.

"Malakai," he breathed, his gaze filled with passion and invitation.

Swallowing my resolve I walked into the room and closed the door. "How is Jon?"

"Better. You saved him."

I nodded, glancing around. It was a very nice room. I avoided staring at the queen-sized bed. "He had no right to take Jon."

"Who is…he?"

"No one you want to know. Listen, I need you to be careful tonight."

"Am I in danger?"

I nodded. "Yes."

His eyes widened. "Why?"

"Because of me, because I care about you, but I won't let anything happen to you, I promise. I want you to do one thing for me. Do not leave this room tonight under any circumstances. Whatever you see in your dreams isn't real."

"My…dreams?" He came closer. "All I see is you. Every night I see you." He touched my cheek.

I closed my eyes. "Don't."

"I want you. I have your blood inside me. I feel you, like you're inside me all the time. Please, Malakai, fuck me."

I took a step back and hit the door. I shook my head, but Jepoi pressed his mouth against mine, forcing me to stop. When he began to fumble with my zipper, I knew I was lost. I wanted him as much as he wanted me, and nothing was going to stand in the way at this moment, not heaven nor earth.

I lifted him in my arms and turned him with his back to the wall. He wrapped his legs around my waist and we kissed again. His kisses warmed my soul, making me want to be inside him so badly, but I held back. My hunger for him and for his blood was gnawing at my soul but it was his pleasure I wanted to stir.

I undid his shirt and kissed down his chest while he stroked my hair. I pulled him off the wall and tore the shirt away, keeping my cursed nature at bay. I didn't want him to see the transformation. It would terrify the bravest of mortals. The last thing I desired was for Jepoi to fear me. But maybe one day, I thought, as I took him to his knees, I would be required to do just that, make him fear me, in order to turn him away...for his good.

He cried out my name as I stripped off his pants and rolled him onto his stomach on the floor. I lifted him easily with one hand, fondling his cock with the other. I parted his perfect backside and made room for my entry. I licked and suckled him, jerking his cock hard at the same time. I heard his cries like a beautiful symphony in my head.

I pulled him to his knees and removed my clothes, stopping every second to kiss or fondle him. I pressed his back to my chest and took him like that, tweaking his nipples and nuzzling his neck. I pumped into him at a steady pace while I stroked his cock so that it stood straight up from his body. I felt my teeth elongate, aware that if Jepoi turned his head now, he'd see my blood red eyes and razor-sharp incisors.

He came in my hand as I continued to fuck him deep and hard then I licked along his jugular and clamped down just at the moment of orgasm. I knew it intensified the sensation because he cried out as his juices ran through my clenched fingers. I drank what I needed and closed the wound perfectly with my saliva.

Jepoi collapsed on the floor, moaning out his pleasure and I reared back, hoping to return to normal before he recovered. Then I heard it. A single word in my head. *No.* I sprang to my feet like a beast whose tranquilly had suddenly been interrupted and glanced around me, on alert. *Where are you?*

How could you?

I am talking to the dead.

Just because you refuse to say my name, my love, does not make me dead. I am still here, and still in your heart.

"Fuck you!"

A hand smoothed over my shoulder now. "Malakai?"

I turned, knowing I was again myself, and smiled at him. "Yes?"

"Who are you talking to?"

"No one." I shook my head. I took him into my arms. "No one at all."

He snuggled close then slowly withdrew. "What you were saying before about my dreams...what?"

"Don't trust them. Even if you think it's me telling you to do something, don't. It's not me." I touched his cheek.

"Who is it? I have a right to know," he said, meeting my gaze.

"Someone from my…past…someone who doesn't like the idea of us being…together, and I need to make this clear." I put my hands on his shoulder. "We can't be together. I came here tonight to warn you not to leave the room. And to tell you…"

"But we are linked. I have your blood in me. I know it. Listen," he breathed, "I don't know what you are, but…you're not like…me, are you?"

I swallowed and shook my head.

"Tell me," he urged.

"I can't. The less you know the better. And please, try and be happy, find someone to love."

He smiled faintly. "I have."

I shook my head.

His expression changed. I think he realised how serious I was.

"You really mean it?"

I picked up my clothes and began to dress.

Jepoi went to sit on the bed. "So who shall I be on the lookout for? Do I need a gun, the police, what?"

"Nothing," I said, doing up my pants. "None of those things will help you. I must remove the one thing that puts you in danger. That's me. They'll have no more interest in you after."

He watched me do up my shirt. "He must be some determined ex-lover. He is an ex-lover, isn't he?"

"Yes, but he's much more than that. It's complicated." I found my shirt. "I will do everything I can to protect you. But you must understand we can't be together like this again."

Tears appeared in his eyes. I sighed inwardly. I wanted to join him but there was no time for sadness.

"Did they hurt you?" he asked.

I paused. "What?"

"After you saved Jon, negotiated with that...whatever it was, did someone hurt you?"

"A routine reprimand." I smiled.

"Didn't sound routine to me. It sounded like torture."

I didn't comment. "I have to go."

He followed me to the door. He reached out and grabbed my arm. I turned and looked at him.

I can't fall in love with him, and a mortal to boot. Oh Heavens.

"I don't fully understand but I'm not giving up."

I leant down and kissed his mouth tenderly. "Sweet Jepoi," I whispered then left while I still had the strength.

As I walked the solemn, rain-ravaged beach, I remembered a different time when Waikiki was a mere swamp and King Kamehameha V kept trying to sell it to rich white men over poker games. He thought it would make a great vacation spot and visualised tourists flocking to it once he turned it into a beach. In 1864 he'd offered it to the Sinclair family for ten thousand dollars but they wanted the island of Ni'ihau instead. He took the cash and though the family still owned the island it was very dry, almost barren.

And Waikiki was an international destination spot.

The Sinclairs and all their heirs must still be kicking themselves.

Thunder kept booming, lightning flashed. The tallest palm trees bent against the wind.

I tried not to think about Jepoi. Even if there was no danger, how could we possibly be together? We could never live a normal life. I would only make him miserable. If I could lose this curse, ask for...mortality? It wasn't the first time that a god had been granted that request after falling for a mortal, but then I wasn't just any deity, I was Kane. I had a greater responsibility than to service my own selfish needs. I was needed to restore balance to an ever demoralised universe.

"You have to find your way back, Kane."

I knew that voice. Before I looked upon him, I glanced up at the moon, praying for self-control.

"You wish to rip out my heart? Too late, you already have."

I sucked in some air, and let my gaze wash over him. He was standing on top of the water, not far from the shore, wearing nothing but a pair of white shorts. Curly brown hair to his shoulders, he was slight and muscular, his face like that of an angel with his large brown eyes. I said nothing, my mouth twisted.

"You still can't say my name."

"Perhaps it's because it means nothing to me," I told him, my voice flat.

"Perhaps," he said softly. "I never stopped loving you."

I pointed at him. "Which is why you betrayed me, unbalanced the universe by sticking a knife in my back and relegating me to...this!" I knew my eyes were glowing unholy red as I stared at him.

"What are you doing here, Kane? You cannot keep him safe by distancing yourself. Let me come home to you."

"And start an unholy war with your master?" I sneered. "I think not."

"I did not approve of him bringing the plague. I begged him to reconsider. He killed many only to get to Jepoi."

I closed my eyes.

"Listen to me, Kane, he is more in love with you than with me. It has always been this way, taking me from you was done in vengeance because you didn't want him. We should join forces, defeat him, topple him from his throne, and you and I could rule this world together."

I shook my head. "You are pathetic. Still, it's about power. You don't want me. You want to take Kanaloa's place."

"That's not true." He was standing in front of me now.

I lifted my arm and pointed. He went flying away from me, landing on his back. I walked over to him and looked down at where he was sprawled in the sand. I waited for him to speak.

"I want both," he spoke. "Is that so wrong? We were meant to rule this world together from the beginning. You know it."

"I know no such thing. You stay away from Jepoi and anyone he knows or loves. Do you understand me?"

"Or what?" He got to his feet, meeting my gaze.

"Or I will tell your master of your ambitions."

His face darkened. "You wouldn't. And he wouldn't believe you anyway."

"He might." I gave him a sinister smile.

He reached out to me. I pushed his hand away. "Don't visit me again." I turned and walked up the beach.

"And still you cannot say my name."

I turned and looked up at the night sky. "Heed my warning—stay away from me and Jepoi..." With that, I gave a huge sigh and shouted, "Delmontre!"

I waited on the beach until the sun almost rose, until I was sure that Jepoi was awake and safe.

When I got back to the house, Felix was waiting. "Thank goodness, you're back, Malakai." He grabbed my hand.

"What is it?" I raised an eyebrow.

He sucked on his finger for a moment.

"Speak!"

"It's the one you can't name and...perhaps others..."

"You mean Delmontre?"

His eyes widened. "Malakai! You said it."

I shrugged. "Yes. I said it. What did you want to tell me?"

"Starzs. He had a visit from Kanaloa. It was not pleasant. Starzs says Kanaloa wants to invoke his doppelganger status. He suspects something is going on with Delmontre. He is requesting your protection."

I began to laugh.

"He's really frightened."

"And so he should be. And why should I give him my protection?"

"He says the stars are aligning, behind you or Kanaloa. He wants to be in your corner. Could be of some use. I advise it."

I sat down in the easy chair and rubbed my chin. Evoking human form and walking among them had always been available to immortals. It was rare they took advantage of it though. My curse relegated me to the human plane. Otherwise, I wouldn't be here either. I wonder what kind of mortal Kanaloa would be, an arrogant one for sure. Delmontre would have less of an issue, his immortal status had been given, not predestined.

When a knock sounded on the door, it jolted me out of my daydream. Felix jumped onto my shoulder and I went to open the door. Starzs stood there. He looked humble. He lifted his sheer house robe. "Hope you've got some human clothes, Kane. I can't walk among the mortals looking like this. I'll get arrested."

I narrowed my eyes. "I didn't agree."

Felix looked around in my face and gave me one of his looks.

I sighed. "Okay, come on in."

As Felix walked in, he bowed his head. "Thank you...master."

I blinked. The game had just begun.

Chapter Five

I was surprised when I awoke in my hotel room a little after seven and heard the news on the radio that the violent storm that had shaken the island of Oahu had passed. The weather had turned warm and balmy. It had raged all night and scared me. It had shaken the windows and sliding doors so hard I thought they might break.

"Gorgeous!" the DJ cackled. "Not unusual in paradise, but very weird after a hurricane-strength wind tore through the island, knocking out power on the west side of Oahu. Maintenance workers say they will have all power restored by noon.

"Just a reminder, folks, some gas stations may not be able to serve you if you are using credit cards. Make sure you've some cash and get an early start."

I got out of the bed and padded over to the sliding glass doors to push back the curtains. I looked out over the ancient Diamond Head. The sun shone so strongly I could see the glittering calcite crystals imbedded in the volcanic tuff cone. It had received its name because of idiotic Western sailors who'd once sailed into Honolulu's harbours and thought the calcite was actually diamonds.

The morning's brilliance hurt my eyes. I'd flown here last night with Jon and hadn't thought about much beyond our emergency situation.

I hadn't had time to think about being stuck here so I didn't have my kit and therefore no sunglasses. I could easily pick up some cheaply along Kalakaua Avenue.

A small bird hopped up on the balcony railing, his head tilted in a hopeful way. Tourists had obviously been feeding him crumbs. I didn't have anything for the poor little guy.

I wondered how Jon was doing. We'd both said to one another at some point that we dreaded being passengers in one of Kimo's planes, but I hoped I'd done right by my friend, that I'd helped him in the worst moments of his crisis.

Then I remembered Malakai coming here and the way he'd fucked me on the floor. My body ached for his touch, but I felt him far, so far away from me.

I glanced at my clothing scattered on a chair and the floor. Jon's blood was on it. I wanted to check with the hospital that my friend was doing okay, but I wasn't sure which one he'd been taken to. Kimo would know.

I retrieved my cell phone and scrolled through it for messages. None. The screen was cracked but the phone seemed to be working. I pondered what to do with my morning. Until I got a departure time from Kimo, I would be free, except I knew I'd have to check out of the hotel by ten. With the reduced rate Kimo got came fewer luxuries such as extra time in the room.

For a moment, I dithered. When had I become so...uncertain about anything? Images of Malakai seeped into my mind, but it was as if he were coming to me from behind a thick veil of fog. I couldn't quite glimpse or feel him. And yet somehow I knew he'd been with me during the night. His essence clung to me.

I wanted him all over me. I lay on my bed for a moment, letting my fingers roam my ass. Yes, he'd fucked me. I felt the passion we'd shared flare through me and I did something I never usually did. I began to stroke my own ass with one hand, jerking my cock with the other. I could still feel his juices on me and inside me. I lifted one leg to make it easier to stick a couple of fingers inside me. I could almost feel his long hair ticking my face and neck as he lowered his body into mine. He'd fucked me as if it would be the last time, as if he were putting out internal fires.

My body arched up to him, I breathed his name, "Malakai." I felt him anxious for closer contact. his mouth and fingers on me. My finger sawed in and out of me. Harder. Faster. I'd never been an anal guy in masturbation, now I yearned for that rigid cock. Yes! That was it. Malakai taunting me, pulling it out to the very edge of my opening, plunging back inside me, push, pull.

God it felt good. I tugged on my cock, heard Malakai whispering my name. I added a second, then a third finger but even these were still no match for his towering member, but my breathing became laboured. I could feel him in me, turning my insides to liquid.

Oh, Jepoi... I could hear him moaning my name in my ear and with one last vicious jerk on my cock, I came all over my hand. When I finally stopped coming, it was a difficult decision to shower. I wanted him in me, all over me.

I walked into the bathroom and turned on the taps. I craved warmth so a hot shower even with horrible hotel soap helped me feel a little less foggy. I dried off and dressed again in the clothes I'd worn the night before.

My gaze fell on the bloody hem of my shirt. *I'll pick up a clean T-shirt on Kalakaua Avenue.* My body seemed different somehow. Leaner, stronger, more sinewy. I couldn't explain it. And yet I didn't feel alert. But then, how could I? Last night had been absolutely fucking horrible, until Malakai had come to me.

It all came back to me. Running into Jon and that man Starzs. The way Evelin and I had followed him then out of nowhere, Jon got hit.

I took a deep breath. Yes. I remembered now. The showdown between Malakai and Starzs over Jon's soul. Almost as if Starzs were the angel of death or something.

Rubbing a towel over my wet head with one hand, I called Kimo with the other. I got his voicemail and left a message. I asked about Jon and let my boss know I was checking out of the hotel and would be down at Waikiki Beach. I had plenty of signal strength and a few bars of battery life. I'd see if I could pick up a new charger at one of the ubiquitous ABC stores. I'd never flown on a job without my kit that had everything I'd ever need, including a second cell phone, backup batteries and extra clothing.

Not to mention a toothbrush and paste. My mouth tasted terrible.

"I'll have my cell phone on. I'm ready when you say the word," I said, before ending the message. I wanted to get home but not badly enough to pay my own way on a commercial ticket. Besides, Kimo wouldn't like that.

As I prepared to leave the room, my plans solidified in my mind. I'd go down to Kalakaua Avenue, grab some coffee, buy a T-shirt and head straight over to the airfield and if I had to, I'd sit in the waiting room until Kimo got me on a flight back to the Big Island. I wasn't sure why but something in me screamed to get back there.

Malakai.

Yes. And no. He might be there, not that I could stroll up to his front door and say, "Hello, let me in. I need to touch you."

I felt, oddly, in danger here. I shook my head. I was losing it. Just because Jon had been in a freaky accident didn't mean I would be too. I just had to hope some recuperating tourist wanted to get back to the Big Island in a hurry to finish his vacation. Otherwise I was on Kimo Time. I could practically hear him saying, "I'll fly you back when I'm good and ready, Jepoi."

Downstairs, I checked out of the hotel, staring at the large painting of Queen Kapiolani mounted on the wall behind it. Though I loved the faded charm of the nineteen fifties' gentility to the place, the painting looked nothing like the gorgeous, gracious queen. Surely they could commission one that seemed a little more like her?

The desk clerk was working on my computer printout, which I'd have to give Kimo. In case there were any discrepancies such as phone calls charged to the room or room service meals, I needed to show him I'd checked out without owing a dime.

When the phone beside her rang, the clerk began an odd conversation and kept saying, "Really?" over and over again. She glanced at me, a strange expression on her face.

I was eager to get going. "Can I go?" I mouthed.

She shook her head. That surprised me.

I waited a moment longer and she ended the call, a troubled expression on her face. She gave me a long look then picked up the phone again.

"What's wrong?" I asked as I heard her ask for security.

Security? What the hell was going on?

A minute later, a burly rent-a-cop arrived. He smelt like *saimin*, the pork noodle soup so popular in the islands. He was still finishing a mouthful and I knew right away he wouldn't be pleasant to deal with. Hawaiians and their food should never be quickly parted.

"There's a problem with your room," the desk clerk said.

The security guard skewered me with a gaze as if assessing how dangerous I might be. I must have read him right because his right hand came up to rest on his utility belt.

"Problem? What problem?" I asked, genuinely dumfounded.

The woman sighed and picked up her phone again. "Matt, can you please come and take over here for a minute?"

A guy in an ill-fitting Aloha shirt came out from behind a door marked *Private* and after giving me a dirty glare, took up his position behind the computer.

"Walk with me," the female desk clerk said. I didn't know her, but I'd worked with Matt before and was a little stunned by his rude behaviour. I accompanied the clerk and rent-a-cop to the bank of elevators. We climbed in and they flanked me. The rent-a-cop began playing with the handcuffs from his belt. Very unprofessional for a security officer but clearly he was a man desperate for power, any kind of power.

The desk clerk glanced at him as he flipped the cuffs back and forth in his hands. He wanted to rattle me. It worked.

On the floor I'd occupied, we exited the elevator and I was surprised to see a group of hotel maids gathered around the door of my vacated room.

"What is it, Maria?" the desk clerk asked.

Maria, a dark-haired Filipina, pointed inside the room. The desk clerk did a double take.

"What the — ?" I gasped when I looked inside. When the hell had this happened? It looked like the San Andreas Fault ran right through the middle of the room. It was split, no, torn in two with a weird smell of earth and rock. I could see what looked like a volcanic fissure with lava seeping over the worn, patterned carpet. That was the smell. A volcanic eruption.

On Oahu?

Diamond Head, the pretty side of the long-dormant Koko Head Crater, had not been active for hundreds of years. I gazed across at the mountain but there was no hint of trouble. It stood serene in the morning light.

This is too fucking spooky...

"You didn't notice this?" the desk clerk yelled. "Oh, my God. I wonder if the rest of the floors have this."

"No. I swear. It's — "

"I'm surprised you were able to sleep." The desk clerk's eyes widened. "How did you sleep through it?"

She took off running for the elevators. She knocked into the security guard who dropped his cuffs. There must have been an island god close because he split his pants bending to retrieve them.

"I'm going to reception," I said loudly. I didn't trust this guy not to arrest me. I walked away steadily as he rose, clutching his ripped pants with a stubby fist.

When I got to the elevator, I heard an enormous crack of thunder and saw a flash of lightning emanate from the room.

I kept pressing buttons, petrified now as the women shrieked and began running.

The security guard's head swivelled in my direction. Holy shit. I banged on the *down* button. An elevator door pinged open. His eyes flew open, a malicious gleam to them. And then he charged towards me.

I jumped into the elevator and pressed the *close* button, but he jumped in before the doors closed. We went down only one floor. Holy crap. Every tourist in the free world was waiting to get on. The smell of lava was strong here.

They were panicking, but I'd started to relax. Nobody could accuse me of having trashed my room. There was no way I could have caused this. I pressed myself back against the far wall as the United Nations that made up Hawaiian tourists flooded the elevator.

It took forever to reach the lobby, but I was surprised to see that though there were some anxious people at reception, whatever had gone on upstairs, the furore hadn't spread through the hotel yet.

"I just called the police," the desk clerk told me as I approached her. "We have no idea what's going on." She bit her lip.

The security guard rolled up, out of breath, sweat soaking his too-tight collar.

"You want me to arrest him?" He jerked his thumb at me.

"Don't be stupid, Jose." Matt, the guy I knew, slid me a piece of paper. "I am so sorry about your stay with us. We hope you'll come again."

He and the female desk clerk were looking at me. Were they kidding? I picked up the piece of paper. No charges. Nothing.

I shrugged. "Laters," I said, the way we said see you later in the island and turned left. Tourists were coming and going, but now, a fresh batch of hysterical travellers from the upstairs floors had begun swarming the desk.

The hotel lobby had no doors or windows. It had been created to look like an old-world Hawaiian hale, fringed by a huge amount of tropical foliage and a low, sloping roof. The space was wide and open, yet the roof easily protected the lobby and its occupants from inclement weather.

It opened, old Hawaiian-style straight onto the driveway where valets took charge of luggage and vehicles. The drivers knew something was up. They all looked distractedly back inside the hotel lobby as I took the short marble stairs down to the driveway and left the hotel.

It was hotter than I'd expected. I felt the ground jolting beneath my feet.

Were we having an earthquake?

I checked my cell phone. No messages. One bar.

Aw, heck. If Kimo couldn't reach me, he'd rip me a new one. I couldn't take a chance. I jumped into a taxi parked outside the hotel and asked him to take me to the airport, to the field offices of Hawaii Air Patrol.

I texted Kimo.

On my way from hotel now.

Since I had only one bar, I couldn't risk making more calls to check on Jon. In case of an emergency I needed to conserve battery power.

I did the unthinkable for me on a working day. I turned the damned phone off.

Kimo stood at his desk, a surly expression on his face when I walked in.

"You took your time," he snapped.

"What are you talking about?"

"Jepoi, I've been calling you for the last hour. The hotel said you checked out two hours ago. Whatcha been doing? Sightseeing?"

"What are you talking about?" I repeated. "I left there about twenty minutes ago." I slid him the computer printout and he opened the folded page.

"A blank piece of paper? What am I supposed to do with that?"

"I—" I snatched the page back. He was right. Blank.

"But I texted you, Kimo."

"Hmm..."

I pulled out my cell phone to prove it to him but couldn't turn it on. No juice. Why did these things happen to me?

When I glanced at the wall clock, I was surprised to see it was ten o'clock. I'd left the hotel at eight. How had I lost two whole hours?

"Where's your kit?" he asked.

"Back on the Big Island." I frowned at him. "We had an emergency last night, remember? Jon's accident? I was off the clock when I called 911."

He shook his head. "Oh. Yeah. Guess I'm outta sorts today."

I suddenly remembered Malakai's warning not to trust people closest to me. I felt myself recoiling. Had he really said this? And did he mean Kimo? My boss sure did seem out of sorts.

He was griping now. "I've never seen you so...disoriented. And what the fuck is up with that blood on your T-shirt? You want to freak out our patients completely?"

"It's Jon's blood." What was with Kimo today? "How is he?" I asked when he ignored my response and slammed around some innocent staplers and pens on the counter.

"Well, he's fine. Doing much better." He pointed a finger at me. "And that's the only reason I'm giving you a free pass today. You helped save his life. So go on and get home. And get some frickin' rest, will ya? The hotel complained about the wild sex you had all night. You and some noisy guy. They said your neighbours complained."

"That is so not true! There was a storm and some kind of earthquake."

He looked at me.

"Is that what the kids are calling hot sex these days?"

"No. Hot sex is hot sex. This was an earthquake. Sure it wasn't on the news?"

He didn't seem to be listening. His glance shifted to some point in the middle distance. "I remember that kind of hot, wild, monkey sex. The kind of sex you only have when you're single. You bein' a *mahu* though, you'll get to have the kinky shit for the rest of your life."

"Earthquake," I repeated. I overlooked him calling me a *mahu* because people in the islands used this word for gay as a matter of course, though we never used it ourselves. Except as a joke. It was derogatory. Extremely derogatory but its roots were so deeply imbedded in Polynesian history it was hard to claim foul with some people.

In Polynesia to this day was an entire culture of *mahu*, men who from birth were designated the female members of the family. Some people saw it as the preservation of culture, but I saw it as a form of slavery.

These young men who grew up in families without enough women to do household chores were forced into women's clothing. They were forced to act and dress and live like women.

I'd seen documentaries on the subject. They became the lovers of men who favoured *mahu*. Some of these young men loved their lifestyle. Very few, as far as I knew, did. I had a crisis point on my hands. I could tell Kimo to go fuck himself and I could go home to the Big Island to a bleak financial future.

Or I could suck it up and move on.

I wanted my job, *and* I wanted to get home. Right now, Kimo was my best choice. I felt like shit. As if I had been tossed around the hotel room like a stuffed toy. As I crept on board the now-waiting plane, I saw Alex at the helm and was relieved to get a thumbs-up from him.

Thank God. At least one person in my world wasn't acting weird.

"Just spoke to the hospital," he shouted above the roar of the engine. "Jon's coming home in a couple of days."

"Great!" I shouted back and buckled myself into a seat.

He could see I was tired and let me sleep. I wanted to get home worse than ever and let my head rest against the cool window beside me. I was trying to remember what kind of sex Malakai and I had enjoyed. I thought he'd fucked me once, but maybe it was more. It seemed to go on and on. Unless that was wishful thinking.

In my memory — or was it my dreams — it had been hot. Sensual. Passionate. But it had never been, in our twilight world, the kind of wild, throwing each other's bodies around the room kind of sex I knew other people enjoyed.

It wasn't my thing, for sure.

When I'd been to nursing school, one of my instructors, Harriet, was a motherly woman my own mom had known for years. She'd recently reunited with her ex-lover from long ago thanks to the Internet. She'd been excited to see him again but when she started showing up with bruises, we all became concerned.

She told us that her lover liked to toss her around, shove her hard against things. She said she enjoyed it, but I couldn't see how. She was covered in bruises. The light seemed to leave her eyes then I noticed the marks on her neck. She'd discovered the fatal pleasures of auto-erotic asphyxiation — the only sexual practice that has an almost one hundred per cent death rate.

Harriet was a nurse and knew the statistics. But her lover was crazy about the practice and apparently, what he wanted, she went along with.

And then she'd died. That was three years ago and I still missed Harriet. She was the perfect nurse. She was calm, reassuring and so knowledgeable. She knew the ways of the ancient Hawaiians and could work with contemporary western and Hawaiian modalities. She had been a gift to us all.

We started to descend and I opened my eyes.

An image of Malakai flashed in my mind. It usually filled me with joy, but I saw him now, his long, gleaming black hair falling over his shoulders, hiding from me.

Another face looked up at me. Harriet.

I almost wept when I saw her face. I hardly ever thought about her anymore, the memory was so painful. She'd been like a mother to me and losing her had devastated me. What sign was I reading from seeing her face?

"Don't trust him," she whispered. "Don't trust a soul."

I focused on breathing as her face became replaced by Malakai's. He reached a hand out to me.

No. I realised now he was pushing me away. That's what he'd been doing when I'd visualised him earlier. He hadn't been calling for me. He'd been pulling himself from me.

So much for hot monkey earthquake sex.

I turned my head, grief swamping me. It seemed fitting somehow that outside, I could see that once again it had started to rain.

At the airport, Alex offered me a ride home and I gratefully accepted. He dropped me out front and I gave him a wave.

I was relieved the house looked normal, though I was surprised that Evelin wasn't home. It wasn't like her. Normally, she was always here. That was another thing. All her paintings of Malakai were gone from the living room. In the hallway, I grabbed my kit and took it to my room, replacing my cracked and spent cell phone with a new one. I plugged the phone into an outlet to charge, got online and ordered a replacement phone for the cracked one. In my line of work, insurance paid when I had to claim for a new phone.

Kimo had said he'd give me the day off, but he'd been known to change his mind. I wasn't tired. For some reason, the short nap on the flight had re-energised me. I felt like a swim. I hadn't felt like a swim in a long time, but for some reason I now had the urge to swim in the ocean.

We had a few local swimming holes that people said were nice, but I longed for the big waves of Kona on the other side of the island. It was over a hundred miles away, but the beach was calling me. I grabbed my kit just in case I'd have to go to work and packed a towel, some water and fruit into a backpack and set off for Kona.

Filling the tank with gas at the Tesco station near the house, I pondered my fastest route and decided I'd take Saddleback Road. The notorious highway got its name because it dipped like a saddle. I'd be able to see the vog from Kilauea and Mauna Kea as I took this journey. I'd shave about five hours off my driving time and almost thirty-five miles taking this highway that cut right through the middle of the island. The US military owned a few installations on the road and discouraged people from using it but being a local, I knew the hot spots. I knew when I could speed and when I couldn't. I knew not to stop anywhere to snap scenic photos unless I wanted the military police to follow me — closely — all the way to Kona.

Back in the car I veered up to the highway and hit Saddleback Road. About twenty minutes into my trip, I was surprised to see Evelin hitchhiking on the other side of the road.

What the hell was she doing out here? I scanned ahead but couldn't see her car anywhere. This was the middle of nowhere.

I would have done a U-turn except that I had a truck right on my tail and the driver began to honk me.

When I checked the rearview mirror she wasn't there. I pulled over, letting the truck pass me.

I had to be seeing things.

I didn't get out of the car but did turn around and the farther I went back, the more I realised I'd imagined seeing her. There was no place she could have gone. Nothing on either side of the road but empty tracts of lava stones from old eruptions. This was a damned spooky place to drive, even during the day.

There wasn't much traffic so I was able to turn around again and I told myself to stop hallucinating. For a moment, I had a terrible sense of fear but then I shook it off.

My cell phone rang.

Alex. I pulled over and took the call.

"You feel like going surfing?" he asked.

"Wow, that's weird. I'm heading to Kona now."

"You're already on your way?"

"Yep."

"Oh, bummer."

"We could meet up there. I don't want to turn around."

"Okay. Only, I know we both have the day off and I figured with the high surf advisory we should try and catch a few waves."

I laughed. "Great minds think alike."

"How far along are you?" he asked.

"I'm on Saddle Road." I hesitated. I wasn't that far along, but I wanted to have my own wheels and I wanted to drive alone.

"Well," I said, "near Mauna Kea." It wasn't a lie but I was a good twenty minutes from actually passing it. "I'm gonna lose reception," I warned.

"I hear ya. Okay, how about we hook up in Kona?"

"Sounds good to me."

"How about Hapuna Beach?" he asked.

The line began to crackle. I'd lose him any second now.

"See you there," I yelled, as if this would make a difference. I moved back onto the road, picking up speed. He'd picked the most popular surfing beach in Kona, but also the most dangerous.

I made good time for about ten minutes until I realised I'd left my surfboard at home. I didn't care. I stepped my foot on the gas and focused on getting to the beach.

Wiki-wiki, as we said in the islands.

At Hapuna Beach, I bought a strawberry shave ice from a food truck vendor. It's a little-known fact to tourists and islanders alike that strawberry was the first flavour of shave ice ever introduced to Hawaii by an enterprising Japanese store owner way back at the turn of the twentieth century. He had a lot of extra ice on hand from selling foods that needed to be kept fresh and he tried to figure out a way to make money off it.

He got the idea of pouring syrup over it and a new craze was born. I stuck my straw in the ice and lolled about outside the truck awaiting Alex's arrival. I'd called his cell phone but had got his voicemail and left him a message.

The strawberry was good. Very good. I found myself savouring the taste. I was hardly hungry or thirsty these days but when I did feel the urge, everything I tasted seemed bigger, sharper, more…sensual somehow. I could taste the berry, so pure and sweet. It was a good shave ice because the syrup went all the way through. I looked down into the paper cone.

Like blood running through veins, the syrup ran in tiny ribbons over the shaved ice.

The thought made me smile instead of shiver.

Weird. Really weird.

I looked up at the sky. Clouds rolled in. On the sand ahead of me, a lifeguard on a skidoo was putting up warning signs for swimmers.

Surfing only.

I could see riptides in the water from where I stood, the waves swelling high in the near distance.

Oh, well. I wouldn't be able to swim here, but I'd wait for Alex.

I glanced to my left and saw Malakai. Man, what a shock. He was beckoning me and I would have followed him anywhere. I was about to walk over to him when I heard a car horn honking.

And there was Alex.

I walked over to meet him. How strange. Alex had forgotten his board, too.

When I mentioned this, he shrugged. "I was in a hurry to catch up with you. You drive fast, man."

I grinned. "I wanted to get over here."

He declined my offer of buying him some shave ice and we walked to the water as soon as I binned my empty cup.

There were a few guys handling the waves, but most got dumped by the choppy water as soon as they got to their feet.

Alex and I stood on the shoreline. I loved the feel of the wind on my face, the smell of the salt spray. The water lapped over my feet.

Frigid. But good. I laughed as the waves frothed on my toes. The lifeguard took off over the sand to another surf break and Alex and I remained, almost alone.

"I didn't think it was going to be this easy," he suddenly said.

"You didn't think what would be easy?"

"Getting you here." He suddenly laughed. What the fuck was he on about? Why did he want to get me here? I knew for a fact, or at least, I was pretty certain he was straight, married and had two kids.

"You don't know?" He had a weird, leering look on his face.

Suddenly, Alex looked like Malakai. Then he was back to Alex again. I stared at him.

Harriet's face came into my mind. "Run!" she screamed. It was all I saw. I felt a sudden sickness, then Malakai's face shimmered over hers.

"Run, baby! It's not me. It's a trick. It's someone else. It's *him!*"

Him? Him who?

The sick feeling was like a cramp so strong it almost knocked me over. "No. I have no idea what you're talking about. This has been the strangest fucking day of my life."

"It's about to get weirder," Alex said, a menacing sneer on his face.

Too late, I tried to run. He suddenly grabbed me and I went facedown into the sand. Water slapped at my head as I tried to kick him off.

"What the fuck!" I screamed, but got his fist in my mouth.

The taste of my own blood only enraged me.

I saw Malakai in my mind, urging me to fight. Alex picked me up, sand, blood, my hair in my eyes.

He threw me into the water, but it was shallow and I landed with a painful thud. I had to get away from him. I knew this, but the pain in my body had left me winded.

I couldn't believe he was doing this to me. We were friends.

He came after me as I tried to get up from the coral bed that had put splinters into my hands and feet.

People were watching. We weren't alone, but nobody came to my rescue as Alex tried to drown me.

I sobbed out of fear and tried to cry out as he dived on top of me, laughing as he held my head under. When I began to see stars, heard the mad, deafening roar of my own blood pressure in my ears I knew this was it.

I was dying.

He was going to kill me.

And I didn't know why.

I turned and bit him hard on the hand. I knew exactly where to bite him for maximum pain. Right near the bone of his forefinger, above the softy, fleshy web separating it from the thumb.

He lashed out at me, but I got in a swift kick to his solar plexus.

Holy mother of... We were getting into deeper water now. I swam as far away from him as I could. He caught up with me, but couldn't quite reach as I fought him off with hard, freestyle kicks.

I have to get out of the water.

When I made my way to shore, the sky seemed black and three men on the beach advanced towards me.

None looked friendly. One of them was the Starzs guy from the night before.

I heard a splash of water and turned. Alex.

Except it wasn't Alex. The next thing I saw was Alex morphing into an image of a shark. Was this real?

The shark rose from the water, steam coming in tendrils from his body.

Not a shark. The shark changed again into a massive, golden-haired man with a shark fin coming out of his back as he spun around in the water.

A shark god.

"Bow before me," a voice intoned, seeming to come out of the sky. "Don't you know a god when you see one?"

How had I displeased the gods?

The shark wanted a sacrifice. It wanted blood.

Mine.

Why? Why me? I was petrified now.

The three men on the beach ran to me, pushing me into the water. I kicked and fought the three men as the shark loomed closer. It swerved right by me—its dead eye wanted me. Waiting for me...to surrender.

Never.

I did something I never thought I'd do. I punched the shark in the head. It reeled back, the three men trying to grapple for me, turning on one another as I got away.

My car was gone. Gone! How the hell was that possible?

I looked for help.

The guy in the food truck hopped into the driver's seat, giving me a panicked look as he took off around the bend.

He'd seen the signs. Seen what was happening.

Somehow, some way, I'd committed *kapu*.

I'd broken a sacred law.

I'm not exactly the most spiritual guy in the islands, but I knew when I was in mega deep shit. And I was in it right now.

He didn't want to help and I didn't fucking blame him. I ran from the beach as fast as my legs would take me.

I was surprised when the food truck stopped in the middle of the road and the passenger door swung open.

Holy heck. What did I do now?

I advanced with great trepidation. Alex wasn't Alex. I'd seen Evelin. But I hadn't seen her. Who was the food truck guy? Friend or foe?

When I reached the door he was almost hysterical.

"Are you crazy?" he screamed. "Get in!" He was crying now. I recognised him.

Jon and I had saved his little boy who'd been shot by pig hunters in the rainforest who got him with a bow and arrow.

"A man with long dark hair came to me and said I'd have to help you. I can't take you far."

He shook with fear as he negotiated the hairpin turns on the road. He was a freakin' wreck.

"It's okay," I said.

"You saved my son. I owe you."

I didn't say anything. I'd get my help where I could, but I didn't believe he owed me a damned thing. He picked up speed and I gathered my wits about me.

Malakai. The long-haired man must have been Malakai.

I began to experience total fear and dread.

"You don't owe me anything," I said, "but you'd better pull over. I don't want them to hurt you. Go home. Forget you met me."

"But—"

"Please," I urged. "They'll catch up with us soon."

"Do you know where to go?" he asked me and something shook my mind. A remembrance I couldn't quite pinpoint.

I knew where to go, but the less he knew, the better.

"Hide up in Captain Cook," I told him. "It's sort of sacred land."

He glanced at me. "A long way from here."

But he stopped and I thanked him as he let me out. I turned to look, but nobody had followed us.

Yet.

I ran through a clump of trees on the side of the road and hid. I waited maybe ten minutes before I saw my car go past, Starzs at the wheel, followed closely by Alex. I waited a long time until I began to get stiff and the coral splinters in my hands and feet began to ache.

Yes. I knew where to go and I prayed that I would make it on time. I limped as the day grew darker and colder until I saw it in the distance and thanked my lucky stars that legends didn't always involve a great lie.

I saw the ancient tiki statues bordering one of the few remaining sacred places for those in need. For those in the kind of trouble that required deep spiritual help.

With hope in my heart and blood pouring into my mouth from my nose and head, I entered *Pu'uhonua O Hōnaunau*, otherwise known as the City of Refuge.

In the time of the ancient kings, anyone who had displeased the ruling monarchs or the deities could come here and seek refuge. None could harm them. As I crossed the invisible line between the outside world and the sacred temple I saw ghosts. Dozens and dozens of men lining the path.

I saw Harriet. And God help me, the Asian woman and little boy I'd seen in the backyard of Evelin's home.

They looked scared. Alone. None spoke. They all looked haunted. Forgotten.

And I had joined them.

I walked with them and they with me. I felt their heavy spirits abiding with me.

And I fell to the ground as the pain and exhaustion caught up with me.

I couldn't see as I felt grass and stone beneath me.

There was just one thing on my mind.

Please don't let me die.

Chapter Six

I watched Starzs plead for mercy without speaking. If I had spoken I swear, I would have opened the heavens above. His whining and snivelling did not impress. It did, however, convince me that Starzs was terrified of me and not involved in the latest events.

Felix had backed into a corner the minute he felt my anger. It was a habit more than anything. He knew full well I'd never hurt him.

I put up my hand as Starzs was about to embark on another tirade of dramatics. He stopped in mid whine when I met his gaze.

A fissure had been created. The portal to the Tiki world had suddenly opened up and swallowed Jepoi, and heaven only knew what kind of creatures had now wandered into this world. "I thought you said they were coming here, that they were going to be walking among the humans?" I demanded as Starzs looked as if he was going to start chanting.

"That's the story I was given. I told you, I received a visit from Kanaloa himself. He was concerned with the activities of Delmontre."

"And speaking of that" — I crossed my arms — "just what did he say?"

"I said I didn't know what Del was up to. That's when he threatened me with things I shudder to repeat."

"Do Ku and Lono know he ventured into this world to check on his fledging?"

"He didn't mention them, master. I think Del is on the run now. Kanaloa wants to revoke his immortal status."

"Good," I said. "Let him do it."

Ku and Lono were among the four great gods. Ku had been married at one time to Hina, a noble goddess, but she lived apart from him, disapproving of his constant demand for human sacrifice.

Lono had once been my good friend. He too had married, contenting himself with music and peaceful pursuits. He often oversaw the growing season. When Kanaloa had started the war, Lono had decided not to choose sides. I hadn't heard from or seen him for ages, and I guess I resented his lack of support.

"So, again, how did you appear there?"

"I told you, Kane, I wasn't there, really. Del must have made himself look like me, then Alex, that other mortal Jepoi hangs with."

Felix approached and took my hand. "What are you going to do?" He looked frightened all of a sudden.

"Jepoi has been dragged into a world where frightening Tiki warriors appear out of the jungle at every turn. There are shark gods and dog gods, men who are part rat and bird. There are human sacrifices there and Jepoi is a sitting target to be the next victim."

"It was orchestrated to make you go in there after him," Starzs bellowed. "It's a trap. Don't go, Kane.

And besides, you can't leave us all alone here unprotected."

I smiled. "I have no intention of it."

"Thank the gods." Felix bowed to me.

"Because you're coming with me." I looked at Starzs who was still on his knees. "Both of you."

Neither one of them said a word. They didn't have to. The fear was written all over their faces.

"How are we going to find the portal, Kane?" Felix asked.

I reached in my pocket and took out the seashell. When I opened my palm, they both gasped.

"You still have it," Starzs murmured. "How? Didn't Kanaloa take it from you?"

"Oh, he tried," I replied between clenched teeth. "Come on, we have no time to waste. We must get Jepoi outta there. Even though he's in the City of Refuge, the longer he stays, the more likely he is to be absorbed into the spirit world."

As we walked down to the water, Felix jumped onto my back and Starzs walked reluctantly behind us. I lowered the shell into the water and the boat rose out of the tide. We walked on board. Felix jumped. I raised my hands and we were headed for ancient mythic Hawaii, the way it was at the beginning, and remained now, hidden from the view of mortals.

I could hardly believe as we sailed the rocky waves Delmontre would go this far. To bring a living mortal here was sacrilege. These portals had been closed for two centuries. There was no way Kanaloa would support those actions. As we drew nearer the portal, I could see the fire-spewing volcanoes in the mist, the surf crashing along the shoreline, and some of the ancient oracles of the Hawaiian kahunas perched on the cliffs watching, waiting for our approach. Carved wooden tikis peered through the rain forest amongst the mystic caves, surrounded by ancient temples where sacrifices were performed daily. Here the honoured dead roamed, slaves to the animal deities they served for eternity, both a blessing and curse, eternal life but never free.

Felix clung to my leg as the ship drifted to the land. I could feel his fear. "I won't allow anyone to hurt you." I turned to look at the dream merchant. There was no colour left in his face in spite of the winds.

When the ship slid up through the sand, I stepped off. I could hear the sounds around me grow silent. They knew. I strolled up the beach to the forest and called out, "Kanaloa. Your whore is out of control!"

Felix tugged on my pant leg. "Decorum, respect."

"None needed." I grunted, pushing him away. "I am his equal, and he knows it." I kept on. "Face me, coward! There is a mortal among us."

Suddenly the ground beneath our feet shook. "Ah." I smiled. "So you heard that one."

From the distance, I saw a flash of white through the trees. I waited. This time both my companions clung to me. Annoyed, I shook them off and sat them a few feet away. "Stay!" I turned and saw him now, floating in my direction, his feet not quite touching the sand. He wore a long white robe and sandals. A gold crown circled his fair hair. It had been a long, long time. I wasn't prepared for the emotion that gripped me upon seeing him again. We'd been close once, like brothers. I wondered if Kanaloa had regrets too.

My first words were those of witticism. I couldn't think of anything else to say. We were face to face now. I let my gaze run over him quite deliberately and announced, "Kanaloa, please, don't you think you've been watching a little too much cinema. I've seen that costume before on another deity."

Kanaloa gave me the faintest of smiles. "All this time, my beloved Kane, and that's all you have to say to me? But then it hasn't been the same around here without your irreverent wit."

"Where is he?"

"Delmontre?"

"To hell with that little twit! The mortal."

"Oh, your little play toy, Jepoi?" He checked his nails.

"Don't tell me you approve of what Delmontre has done!"

"Can't say that I do given his..." He glanced up and met my gaze. "...motives."

"Whatever they may be, he has exploited the power you bestowed on him. Take it away. Make him mortal again."

"Make him mortal?"

"Strip him of power! Yes."

"I prefer to strip him period. He is a sublime submissive. I'm grateful the way you taught him to obey like that, Kane."

"You talk stupidity!" I was losing my patience. "Delmontre has made a joke of you."

"Oh, I wouldn't go that far. I have wondered, however...this curse I gave you, the...ah...vampire thing, I hear the sex is...well..."

"Okay," I interrupted his rambling impatiently, "if you won't help me look for him, I'll do it on my own."

Kanaloa shrugged. "Do as you like, but you do it at your own peril. You have been banished from this world. Everyone knows it. I rule this world now. If you enter, you may never leave."

"There's nothing else you can do to me, Kanaloa."

"You'd be surprised." He smiled. "We could stop all this in a heartbeat. I would send your human home, and you could help me find Del, and discipline him for me. We'd rule together, the way we were meant to." There was appeal in his expression.

"I will never rule at your side again. One day, you will grovel at my feet."

He laughed. "We'll see."

"If you know where he is…" I threatened.

"The truth is, I don't. He's hiding. He has your blood which has given him more common sense than most humans. When he saw the dangers around him, he took shelter."

Kanaloa turned his attention to Starzs now. "And you, I warned you, vermin, to stay out of this."

Starzs was prepared to grovel, but I held him back. "He is mine now. Touch him at your own risk. Don't think just because you've cursed me to eternal darkness and banished me from ruling this world I don't have power still."

Kanaloa took a step back. He inclined his head. "Go on with your ragtag worshippers, Kane, but be forewarned, I don't play fair."

I walked by, my companions hiding behind me as they too scurried by.

"When you see that ex slut of yours," Kanaloa called out, "tell him I said you could have his sorry ass."

I didn't reply. Truth was, I didn't want his sorry ass or any other part of his anatomy. All I wanted was to get Jepoi out alive. I was hoping that having my blood in his veins might make those who would attack him think twice, but it was only wishful thinking.

Starzs' voice woke me from my meditation. "You can communicate with him."

I glanced at him then all around me, looking for the slightest movement. "Yes, but there are those here who could hear, lead them right to Jepoi."

Starzs put his finger to his lips. "Yes, but...I have an idea."

Felix moved closer, hopped on my shoulder to listen.

"Go on," I said.

"I don't know if I could hold it long, but during your communication I could put everyone into a dream state."

"The entire island?"

"Yes, but not for a long time, just long enough for you to get a message to the mortal, and find out where he is."

"Splendid! Go ahead. Do it now."

"Get ready to contact him in your mind, Kane. And no time for niceties. Get right to it."

"I'm ready."

"Take my hand," he said.

I took it and Felix clung to me.

Suddenly in front of me was a hazy glow. I conjured Jepoi in my mind. *"Jepoi, it's Malakai. Please tell me where you are. I'm here. I'm coming to get you. Where are you?"*

"Malakai?"

"Yes. Where are you?"

His voice was faint, but I could hear it. *"Malakai? I don't know where I am. Where am I? Why is this happening?"*

"No time for that now. Describe your location."

"Cave...rock...water...water..."

"Jepoi. Stay with me. Waterfalls? Are you in a cave near a waterfall?"

He was gone. The haze lifted.

"I couldn't hold it any longer," Starzs admitted. "Kanaloa was fighting me the entire way. Did you contact the mortal?"

"Yes, Jepoi told me he was in a cave near a waterfall. There are many caves and many waterfalls on this island so we'll need to check each one until we find him! Come on."

I knew the way would be treacherous. Kanaloa was not just going to sit back and let me have free reign. Already he'd called up the dead Tiki warriors and was readying them for battle. I had no weapon, and the two I had with me were not soldiering material.

I warily moved through the thick jungle, my entire body tensed, prepared for attack. My immediate needs were twofold, I needed to feed in order to be at maximum strength and I needed a weapon.

Suddenly I stopped as I heard the joyous sound of someone yelling out... Whew! It was not unheard of here for someone to go sledding down a volcano at fifty or more miles an hour. I started to run towards the sound.

Felix was holding me around the neck so tightly, he was choking me. Starzs was trying to keep pace and swearing profusely. Finally I stood at the bottom of the giant volcano. I reached out my hand and grabbed hold of the creature, half snake and half something resembling a mortal. In its belt was a small dagger. I ripped it off him and dropped it in my pocket then I bit into the fleshy beast and drank my fill.

The blood was rich and nourishing. The creature died and I dropped what was left of the scaly carcass then moved forward again.

"That was simply...disgusting and yet kind of sexually invigorating at the same time," Starzs sang out, stepping over the corpse.

I rolled my eyes and wiped my lips.

"That's what I mean about being a great dream subject," Starzs was saying to Felix who was navigating the ground now. "People love sex and gore."

"Where did you read that?" I muttered.

"I know it. I'm a dream merchant, remember?" Starzs scoffed. "I know what your innermost desires are."

"Good," I said. "Use it and find Jepoi."

"You love him," he accused.

I paused and turned to stare at him. "Are you insane?"

"No. I know your dreams. The great Kane is slave to his heart...and that heart belongs to a mortal."

Felix was staring at me now, his mouth hanging open. "Say it isn't true, Malakai, please? I thought you were over him."

"It is impossible," I grumbled and moved forward. But I'd questioned it myself, hadn't I? Just irked me that Starzs had to know anything about it.

"Just like Del."

Starzs went on as I pushed the brush out of our way so that we could move towards the upcoming waterfall.

"He is in love with Kane, has always been, but he was seduced by power. After the glitter fell out of his eyes, all he could see was Kane. Now, he's desperate, and desperate men do desperate things."

I paused and let my eyes close for a minute. That meant that he could kill Jepoi in a blink of an eye. I had to find him now. The two chattering behind me were beginning to grate on me. I swooped up Felix and said, "Okay, quiet. I need to concentrate."

The waterfall was a rainbow of colour. I could feel the spray of water already as I approached. I scanned the area for a cave and realised there was one under the rainbow where there was just enough room to pass without getting soaked. "Hurry," I said, feeling the trees around us come alive with movement.

I froze when I heard voices murmuring, like a drone of bees, flying straight for us. I withdrew the dagger, thinking maybe this was my opportunity to secure at least a sword, and told Felix and the dream merchant to hide.

In the sky above me were what looked like flying dogs with brilliant yellow eyes, their heads brimming with jagged, menacing teeth. I counted at least ten and as they attacked, I went into defence mode, killing one with the dagger as I ripped out the throat of another with my teeth. Very quickly, all ten lay dead or dying. I motioned to my companions and we hurried through the watery corridor to the door of the cave.

It was only after we entered, I knew Jepoi wasn't there. Right inside was a huge drop. I lifted up before being swallowed and grabbed the other two, preventing them from spiralling off into oblivion. "There's nothing here but death," I said and as I turned, Felix and Starzs to either side, a door slid closed over the cave door plunging us into darkness.

Felix immediately began to panic as did the merchant. "Quiet," I told them. "They forget, I have formidable night vision." I slowly turned to see that there was solid ground on the other side. We had no choice but to carry on in the cave, perhaps find another exit. "Hold on," I told them. I gave a great leap and took to the air, only to land safely on the other side.

I put down the two and glanced around.

Felix clutched my pant leg. "I have Starzs by the hand. He can't see anything either."

"Calm yourself," I said. "For now, we are alone." I'm not sure how long I wandered through the winding corridors of that cave. I could hear water trickling from somewhere which meant there was another waterfall close, but I couldn't seem to find my way out. Then I heard the music.

I smiled, a burst of joy breaking in my heart and I told my companions to hurry.

"Where are we going?" Felix asked.

"The Festival of the Makahiki."

In front of my eyes, it appeared, the great Olympic-like games, the chiefs regrouping their forces, the citizens lining up to pay taxes. To dance, celebrate, no work, no war. *Lono.*

Felix was aware and as light was everywhere, he glanced around with wondrous eyes as Starzs exclaimed, "But it's only June!" The festival always took place between the months of November and February.

I scowled at him. The guy was seriously an idiot. It didn't matter the month. Lono had come to help us, guide us towards the entrance. I wandered into the centre of it all. The harvest had been abundant. The people feasted, and danced, and copulated. Babies cried and children screamed in play.

I looked for Lono. I didn't see him, but I did see Laka, his bride, dressed in a rainbow gown, beautiful flowers in her hair. She came to greet me, kissing my face. She pointed beyond the festivities. There was the door and I could see the flashing colours of yet another waterfall. "Lono sends his greetings," she whispered.

It disappeared behind us as we moved to the exit. I stepped through, bidding the other two to follow. The force from the waterfall toppled Felix and he went rolling down a small hill. Starzs ran to fetch him, but Felix was able to steady himself and levitate. I sought the entrance to the cave.

A great wind howled suddenly from above and a current began pulling me at a dizzying speed towards the caves entrance just beside the waterfall. As I tumbled inside, I lost sight of Felix and Starzs. When I turned around, I was no longer in a cave but in a luxurious room with a big round bed and silk sheets in the palest of yellow. The walls all around me had no door, and no window. A trap? Had Lono been part of this, or was he just a pawn? I placed my hands at specific points along the wall. They were solid concrete. I was contemplating the best way to bust through when I heard a voice say, "It's for the good of us all, my love. You know that."

I turned around to see Delmontre lying naked on the bed, his thighs spread wide, wrists cuffed over his head. His body had been thoroughly oiled. I could smell the intoxicating scent of musk mixed with roses.

"I'm yours, Kane, just the way you like. Come here and possess me. I am nothing without you."

"You are nothing anyway," I scowled. "Kanaloa should take away your power. You are like a child with a toy he's not quite sure how to play with."

"I was destined to be a god. I am descended from your kind."

"You're a cousin three times removed who, if not for your obvious…" I let my gaze fall on his long, hard sex, which glistened with a mix of oil and pre-cum, "assets, would have ended up a slave in this world. Let me out of here, Delmontre."

"I know you want me, how can you not?"

It was true, the sight of him like that was seductive. It was not seductive enough, however, to make me forget what I'd come here for. "I no longer want you. And if I ever take you again, it would not be with mercy."

"Then indulge, my beautiful Kane, possess me with all you have, fuck me for eternity. I will take all you have."

"Ha!" I laughed at him. "You couldn't take a quarter of it. Now, tell me how to leave this room or I will rip the walls down, one by one. Your choice."

"What do you see in that mortal?"

"I am responsible for his well-being."

"You feel more than that. And even if you achieve what you've come here for, do you really think I'll give up, just let you go to his bed? I have many eyes on the outside. You'd be surprised."

"You think? I know you stole Alex's soul, not to mention Jon's."

"Jon? No, he's fine."

"You lie. You use his body whenever it suits you."

"Jepoi and Jon will be lovers, and Alex will be their lover too. Jepoi won't have time to think of you."

"Is that your plan?"

"Yes, because Jepoi has your blood." He lifted his hips a few times. "He is too hard to kill, but he's not hard to seduce. Mortals are far more easy than gods."

I turned to the wall, plunged my fist into the concrete then I started ripping the walls apart.

The scenario disappeared behind me and the first thing I saw was Felix peering at me. "Where'd you go?" he asked.

"Don't ask." The walls deteriorated around me and we were back at the waterfall. "Where's the damn cave?"

"Starzs found it over there," Felix pointed.

I could feel Jepoi now. "I'm coming," I called out.

Inside the cave, Starzs waited. "He's here somewhere, isn't he?" he asked.

I nodded at him. "Jepoi, it's Malakai, where are you?" We roamed the inside of the cave for a few minutes then I heard him.

"Malakai, is that you?"

I turned to see Jepoi come out from behind a stone wall. "Jepoi!" I was so glad to see him.

He ran to me and we embraced. I checked him over with my eyes. He was battered and bruised. I could take care of that later. "Are you well?"

"I'll be okay," he said, looking curiously at the others, "I… Where are we?"

"Ah," I began, not sure how to explain it.

"I thought I was in the City of Refuge and then everything changed. It was so weird. "

"Allow me to introduce myself." Starzs stepped forward. "I'm ah…dream…"

"He's a merchant," I intercepted, "sells…ah…sleep accessories."

Starzs shot me a look.

"Oh," Jepoi said with his eyes on Felix, who jumped on my shoulder, "hello."

"This is Felix," I said. "He's my friend."

"Pleased to meet you." Jepoi held out his hand.

Felix shook it briefly then said loudly in my ear. "Can we dispense with the niceties, Kane…I mean…" he smiled at Jepoi, "Malakai, and get the hell out of Oz?"

"Oz?" Jepoi said. "Malakai, what is going on? This place is really…it's like nothing…where in the hell are we?"

"In a dream," Starzs murmured, nudging me, "a dream that's about to become a nightmare in about twenty seconds."

"Damn!" I exclaimed. I grabbed Jepoi's arm. "Come on, we need to find another exit. They've found us?"

"Who?" Jepoi asked breathlessly, running beside me. "What do they want with me? I've done nothing and…"

"It's not Kanaloa's army," Starzs announced when the echoing footsteps came ever closer. "He's saving those until last. It's a combination of rat and dog small-fry gods."

"We need swords," I said, dragging a breathless Jepoi to the wall along with the other two. "Do they have swords?"

Starzs had the power of being able to see the immediate future so he could see them approach. After concentrating a little, he said. "They all have swords. There are at least twenty of them. We can't fight them, Kane…I mean…Malakai," he corrected. "There are too many."

"Listen, take Jepoi ahead with you. Find the exit. I will follow."

Jepoi grabbed my shirt. "No. I'm not going without you. And why does that mattress salesman keep calling you Kane? Kane was the god of…" He sucked in some breath and shook his head.

"Never mind that," I said. "He's quirky like that. Just do as I say. We'll make it." I kissed the top of his head. "Take him," I told the others.

As Jepoi was dragged forward under great protest, I leapt to the top of the cave and waited. It wouldn't be easy, but at least I had the power of surprise. I could use some help here.

"*Ku?*" The god of war, another cousin who, like Lono, preferred to now live the quiet life with his bride Hina. "*Ku-Ka-ili-moku…we have in the past looked down on your dark practices, but we are kin. Help me now before someone like that half cast mortal steals more power from his weak-willed lover. If you want sacrifice, my friend, come…I will have plenty for you.*"

"*You assume, Kane, I still have taste for war.*"

"*You do not?*"

"*You can no longer see the sun and yet it was you who once filled the universe with it. I find it quite…ironic.*"

"*You are not alone.*"

"*Now you need my dark powers?*"

"*I ask for your solidarity. Your price was always high, my brother, but your instincts were right on.*"

I caught a glimpse of them below and swooped down. I killed two and secured their weapons. I killed two more and they kept coming. I sliced with the swords through the air and then looked up to see Ku staring at me. He winked and let out a yell. Together, we struck them to the floor of the cave. He left enough alive for his sacrifices, ordering two slaves to whisk them away.

We both touched down on the cave floor. He swept his gaze over me. "Kane."

"Ku," I bowed my head at him as he did to me. "You have my gratitude."

"And you do this all for love?"

"The universe is out of control. Kanaloa has let that little shit steal his power. He has already stolen souls."

"All for love as well."

"That's not love."

"We all knew the mortal made a mistake choosing Kanaloa over you. And look at what it has brought."

"Then fight at my side. Lono will not take part, given his heritage. He will restore peace only at the end."

"On one condition, brother," he said. "We take down Kanaloa for good."

"Displace him?"

"He's out of control. I offered to help you at the time of the division, but you refused. He should have never been allowed to delve in dark magic to make you what you are. The council is useless against him. They fear him. But the one person Kanaloa fears most of all is you, Kane. And that pissant ex-slut of yours knows that when another battle comes, you will emerge the victor."

"How could he...unless..."

"Yes," Ku nodded. "He has paid to see the future."

"Starzs?"

"Worse, Deacon Veil."

"Then he's real?"

"Afraid so. He wanted to make an alliance with me some time ago. He's too foul even for me. But he sees the future. He can't affect it directly, but he can manipulate it. He told me you would regain your place eventually and I know that little worm, Del, has visited him on many occasions. He pays with his...ah...charms?"

"That I believe," I muttered.

"Leave here now, Kane. Take your human. It's dangerous. The exit is straight ahead. We will be in touch." He lowered his head in respect and was gone.

Jepoi was waiting at the exit of the cave. I was amused to see that Felix had hopped on his shoulder. He clutched my arm and dragged me closer when he saw me. His mouth smothered mine and the sky above grew dark and thunderous.

"Oh boy!" Felix muttered. "Kane...Malakai...let's...
go!"

"I missed you," Jepoi said. "I was so worried."

I squeezed his hand. "Don't worry for me. Let's go."

Felix hopped back to me and we ran, headed for the water. Jepoi mentioned something about there not being a ship and Felix replied. "There will be!"

Just as we reached the shore, a huge wave blew up in front of us and there was the army of dead warriors. Kanaloa's army.

We stumbled back as they marched on us. I had no choice. I would have to use the power I had to command them, to change their course, even though I was breaking a sacred rule...revealing my power to a mortal.

"Kane! Do something!" Starzs hollered.

I raised my arms out in front of me and chanted in the ancient tongue. I asked the sea to reverse and at the same time, I tossed the shell into the water. The wave turned back and the army spilled into the ocean. I caught a quick glimpse of Ku. He'd added his power to mine to help me. As the wave turned over yet again, our ship came with it, and settled onto the calm waters.

Jepoi looked stunned, but there was no time now to explain. We ran into the water, dragging him with us, and boarded the ship. I checked the skies. Dark, murderous clouds loomed above us. Kanaloa would not make it easy for us to get back. But I knew Ku was somewhere in the background. I would owe him. I turned the boat in the right direction and we began to move forward. Then the skies opened like a giant dam, drenching us.

"Get Jepoi below," I told Felix. "Stay there, all of you!" I shouted as I gripped the wheel, my hair and clothes clinging to my flesh.

The ship rocked and danced on the treacherous waves as the thunder and lightning ripped through the skies. I laughed like a god gone mad as I spotted the divide between the two worlds then I sent my own thunderbolt upward. It split the night in two, and the darkness crumbled as the ship floated peacefully through the door of the living world.

My three passengers raced up to the deck. Jepoi ran to me as Starzs and Felix acted like happy clowns in a circus.

Jepoi clung to me. He looked up, pushed back some of my long wet hair. "Poor you, you're soaked to the skin."

He kissed me again as I steered us to shore.

Jepoi shielded his eyes from the sun and spied my house. "It is real!" He turned to me. "I thought I'd gone mad. This is your house."

"Yes," I said. "It's my house."

Starzs carried Felix off the boat and they headed to the house. Jepoi didn't let go as we walked off the deck. I knew the ship would disappear behind us, but there was nothing I could do to prevent him from noticing.

We stopped and he looked at me. "You need to tell me everything."

"I will."

Jepoi went to say something else then he turned to the water. "The...ship. How did that...it just disappeared like you made it appear and..."

I put a finger on his lips. "Let's go in. I promise I will tell you what I can soon."

We went inside. Felix offered Jepoi a drink while I went to my room and towelled off. After I was dressed, I found some dry clothes, and offered them to Jepoi. He was sitting in the living room with Felix and Starzs, sipping hot chocolate.

Jepoi took them with a quiet thank you.

Felix and Starzs suddenly left the room, leaving me alone to talk to Jepoi. I sat opposite him by the fire, not sure how to begin.

He looked at me. "I really don't need these" — he indicated the clothes — "I'm not the one who got wet."

"You might like a change later, that's all."

He shrugged. "I guess. Am I staying?" He met my gaze. "Kane? Malakai? What is your name, really?"

"Kane," he said. "Kane Milohai."

I laughed.

"Why is that funny?"

"Who named you that? It was a joke? It means 'man', you know."

"I know what it means."

"I saw some things...where were we exactly?"

"Hawaii...just on the other side."

"The other side of Hawaii? It didn't look like California to me."

"I meant to say...another side of..." I broke off. "Jepoi, listen to me. I don't want you to trust anyone from now on, even your closest friends, Jon or Alex. Do you understand?"

"What? Are you out of your mind? Why shouldn't I trust my friends? I mean the thing with Alex...that was freaky, sure, but — "

"They're not always what they seem. They may look familiar, but it is what's inside that's...not what you expect."

"I can't understand what you say. That's rich, coming from you, Malakai, or Kane, or whatever your name is. Someone tried to kill me. I made my way to the City of Refuge. I felt guided there... Then suddenly I'm on this island and nothing is...real...it's impossible what I saw. And you tell me not to trust what's inside my friends. What about what's inside you?"

I moved over and sat in front of him on a stool. I touched his face and watched the cuts heal. "If I'm not completely honest with you, Jepoi, it's because I can't be. The more you know about me, the more dangerous your life will be."

"Can it get any more dangerous? I know you're not...you're a mystery...you have powers that...I know you're not like me...and where I was, it's like nowhere on this earth. I saw...people with heads of dogs and rats and...made no sense, like I was walking into a mythological story."

I didn't comment. Instead, I went to reassure. "I won't let anyone hurt you, but we mustn't see each other anymore."

"No. Malakai...Kane...please, I love you."

I glanced around me. "Don't say that aloud. Listen, you must promise to be wary of everyone, even those you call your friends. Is that clear?" I stood. I couldn't endure his words of love. It made me weak, and I wouldn't put his life in danger because of my weakness for him. "Come," I invited. "You must be hungry. We'll eat then I'll take you home."

Jepoi clung to me. "Don't make me leave you." He kissed me again. I was lost for a few seconds until that voice inside me pulled me back. I managed to get disentangled. "I'll see about some food," I muttered and walked off.

In the kitchen, Felix had already begun to prepare a meal. He was heating up his homemade pasta sauce. He saw my face and came to touch my hand. "It will be fine. It is best he not understand."

"I know. But Del warned me about being in Jon and Alex's body. He will use them like puppets."

"If it's just sex, and he doesn't hurt Jepoi..." He paused. "Let him go, Kane. You have no choice. Look at the trouble today, for him and you."

"Ku will fight with me. He is one of the reasons we survived. And Lono helped me as well today."

"Ku? Ku helped us. He frightens me, Kane."

"Yes, but not as much as Deacon Veil."

"Deacon Veil?" Felix dropped the spoon he was using to stir the sauce. "He's the...devil."

"Um," I nodded. "Apparently, Del has been asking favours from him, as well as fucking him as payment."

"Yuck." He picked up the spoon and rinsed it in the sink.

"My thoughts exactly. But if Delmontre will fuck Veil, he'll do just about anything, won't he?"

Felix appeared to shudder.

Chapter Seven

Once again I found myself expelled into the cold. This time, however, it devastated me. Malakai's house had been my only real refuge. A house also, of secret pleasures. I knew, just *knew* that Malakai enjoyed having me there. I knew that Malakai loved me. I knew this not out of ego, but a soul-sense. Malakai had looked at me with so much love, even as he'd said those hateful words, *we mustn't see each other anymore*.

I took a deep breath as Malakai sort of evaporated. Yeah, that was the only word for it. He dissolved into atoms and I could have convinced myself I'd hallucinated or imagined it. I walked down the driveway of Evelin's property and entered the house through the back door.

She was in the kitchen, drinking red wine, painting butterflies as was her wont, but these ones had evil red eyes like...like vampire bats and their wings were steel-tipped bats' wings. They were utterly gorgeous, yet disturbing creations.

"Where have you been?" she asked.

"How long have I been gone?"

She looked at me. "What do you mean? You've only been gone all day. Your boss called twice looking for you."

"He gave me the day off. I went surfing."

Evelin gave me a faint smile as she shook her head. "As usual, Kimo changed his mind. He said your cell phone voicemail messages were full and you weren't returning texts. The police called and said your car was found abandoned in Kona and Alex, the pilot, he went missing, too."

I swallowed. Just remembering the crazy things that had happened when Alex called me, asking to surf then trying to kill me. I could still taste Felix's pasta sauce on my tongue. Oddly, it gave me comfort, warmed me at the memory of the morning... Man, it seemed like months ago that I'd been fleeing the man I thought was my friend.

Felix's pasta was like nothing I'd ever tasted before. I almost giggled thinking about how Malakai, Felix and the crazy Starzs could traverse the other side of the rainbow — because I was certain now that this was where Malakai had collected me from — then turn right around and make pasta for dinner.

"Anyway," she said, painting an extra deep red on the tips of her butterfly-bats' wings, "I had Triple A tow your car back here. He says you're going to have to work the next six days straight for having today off."

"Oh, joy." I shook my head. Kimo would never let me hear the end of taking the day off today and I already dreaded his grumbling and groaning.

"I made some pasta. Are you hungry?"

"No, but thank you."

"Oh, come on, sweetie. You need some meat on your bones. You can't survive on red wine and good cheer."

I didn't argue. Evelin took her culinary skills seriously and everything she knew she'd learned from Mario Battali's cooking shows. I accepted a plate of rigatoni and took a bite. Fantastic, though not quite as magical as Felix's cuisine.

Magic.

The thought hit me. Yep. Malakai was some kind of conjurer...no, more than that. Some kind of ethereal being. Whenever I came close to figuring it out, Malakai seemed to throw up a beautiful wall of seductive fog. I would get visions of the two of us making love. Sometimes it seemed real, sometimes a haunting, achingly beautiful fantasy.

I sighed.

"What's the matter? Don't you like it?"

I shook my head and she looked alarmed. "No, it's wonderful," I assured her.

She smiled then, but I was in a world of hurt. I felt heartsick that Malakai had made me leave. It was always like this with guys. Gay ones, anyway. I hardly ever heard of women throwing men out of their homes, but I knew of straight men who asked women to leave as soon as the sex was over.

Evelin had a date like that once, where the man asked her to leave. She'd called me in the middle of the night and I'd driven over to pick her up. She'd cried the whole way home. It had shocked me at the time that she was no spring chicken, and frankly, neither was he, but he had acted like a callow youth.

Unbelievably, I'd always hoped to run into the guy sometime so I could give him a piece of my mind, but when I did, he'd been in a terrible accident and I'd had to nurse him on the plane to Honolulu.

I'd never told Evelin the story. I was afraid she'd be hurt, or worse, that she'd be royally pissed that I'd helped keep him alive instead of stepping on his oxygen tube or something.

Malakai was different. There was something otherworldly about him. I had deluded myself in matters of the heart in the past, but this was different. Oh, I was still capable of self-deception, who wasn't? But I knew with unwavering certainty that Malakai was the man for me.

Okay, so I didn't understand everything that had happened. Didn't understand the ship that had taken me from real life, crossing the borderline between the seen and unseen. I didn't understand how I'd been rejected by the inhabitants of the City of Refuge and somehow crossed the rainbow and survived, but I knew one thing.

Malakai had come for me because he *loved* me.

He'd done this with no sense of obligation or moral duty. I saw fathomless, ageless grace in Malakai's eyes. Sensed his deeply lonely existence. I didn't care if it took me a lifetime, but one day, Malakai and I would be lovers. We would be partners in every sense of the word. We would be together in that incredible house and neither of us would be alone anymore. We would be whole, never to be parted again.

I bit my lip, wondering if all these deep thoughts, which were not the norm for me, had anything to do with my near-death experience. I'd never felt quite the same since, and almost cried out at the sense of joy, the little prism of hope lying buried in my soul. I'd always known…somehow, that I wouldn't be with anyone ordinary. I knew I'd find someone artistic, different.

And Malakai sure as hell was different.

Evelin handed me a glass of wine. I sipped. It tasted very good. I took another bite of her pasta. I could taste all the flavours. She'd made it with eggplant and tomato, basil and something else.

"What's in this?" I asked.

"What does it taste like?"

I reeled off the ingredients and she nodded. "I'm drawn to red lately so my secret is the pimento from green olives."

Taking another bite, I nodded, savouring another explosion of flavour. This was more than I'd eaten in weeks. "I love these new butterflies," I said. "They look like bats."

She laid down her very fine paintbrush, swept a strand of hair over her ear with the back of her hand and said, "You're going to think I'm crazy, but I swear it's true."

"What?" I stood, leaning against the counter, a memory flashing in my mind of coming home one night to find Malakai doing this. It almost shattered me to think of it, but it also fortified my focus.

Making Malakai mine.

"Tell me." I picked up my wine and sipped.

"It started a few hours ago. These butterflies, except they weren't, they just *looked* like butterflies until I got a closer glimpse of them, they were more like batterflies, hybrids of bats and butterflies, showed up in the garden. Hundreds of them."

I didn't say anything. I wondered if Malakai had sent them to her, to protect Evelin and the home she and I shared.

"When did they leave?" I tried to keep my tone casual.

"Well..." She stared at me. "Wait...you're not surprised?"

There was silence between us for a moment. Outside, I could hear the faint but distinctive singing of a *coqui* frog.

"Ah," Evelin said, "they're back."

I smiled. "You mean they left?"

She nodded. "As soon as the batterflies arrived. It was the strangest thing. They just turned up." She glanced from side to side. "I took a photo of them." Her tone was hushed, almost frightened. I was stunned when she showed me the image on her camera phone. She was right. I could make out the fiery, red eyes, the unusual wing tips. I stared at her.

"There were more," she said. "They've all disappeared. I'm glad you've seen it otherwise if this one vanishes too then I'll accept it was a hallucination. But I just know it wasn't."

No. Not a hallucination. One more piece of evidence that Malakai wanted me to know he was real. That *we* were real. I had no doubt the picture would vanish, but I felt exhilarated now. Malakai couldn't quite turn me away, push me out of his life. The bats were his.

And he... I took a sip of wine.

He was some kind of a god. A vampire god.

I shook my head. I was doing a lot of that since I'd walked in the door, but then it had been a weird day. A weird few weeks. Nothing seemed the same. Nothing felt right except when I was with him. I'd been so consumed with being around Malakai again that I hadn't taken in much of my surroundings. Now I thought about it, his home, I recalled it had been filled with antiques. Rich, red velvet curtains that shrieked of opulence. Ancient *koa* wood furniture that was only handed down family member to family member these days. Ancient idols that I just knew weren't reproductions. The house had been filled with paintings and objects of art that were valuable.

But they were hybrids of art.

He had pieces of bygone eras sacred to our islands. Representations of our gods that Queen Ka'ahumanu had ordered destroyed upon the death of her husband, King Kamehameha the Great. She had demolished the old, fearsome patriarchal order, banished the powerful island gods.

It had been said that even as she ordered all the sacred *heaius*, temples, destroyed, loyal devotees had hidden the tikis. Some were on display in the Bishop Museum and some were still kept secret by some of the islands' oldest families.

So, Malakai's people had been here a long, long time.

I thought about Ka'ahumanu, who had destroyed our way of life. In liberating her people from a strict *kapu*, a system of taboo that was way too easy to violate, she had destroyed the fabric which had woven us all so tightly together.

When I thought about what I'd seen of the old Hawaii, it was beautiful but dangerous. King Kamehameha the Great had forbidden women, even his many wives, from consuming certain foods. Even fruits were off limits to them except during funerals. Women and men couldn't eat together or sleep together.

His favourite queen, Ka'ahumanu, had changed all of that and embraced Christianity, with disastrous results. The men who brought her their unfamiliar god, also brought a different set of rules. A whole new system of *kapu*. The Hawaiian way of life, which operated with the rhythm of nature, became unacceptable. The way our people dressed, the food we ate, the way we lived, was suddenly wrong.

But Malakai wasn't like that. I knew that. He straddled two worlds. The living and the dead. He had power and knowledge and used them for good.

He was a powerful being lying in wait.

Yes. His home was a hybrid of cultures.

Just like him.

Kimo called me a little before seven. I was utterly exhausted, but it was that awful kind of exhaustion where you are so tired you just can't sleep. I would sleep for an hour and waken. I'd stare at the clock. Time just crawled by. I couldn't stand it. I wanted to get up and make use of my time, but when I closed my eyes, I couldn't sleep. It wouldn't have been so bad if Malakai had been waiting for me in dream, but he wasn't. I saw him in shadows. Heard his voice. Tasted his kisses. He was there. Not there. At dawn I felt him hovering over me. I opened my eyes and he was gone. I could have wept, but I was too tired even to do that.

I'd been aware all night of Evelin not sleeping. She'd paced the house. She sometimes did that when she was painting. When I'd first moved in, man I'd forgotten all this, but the first night I was sleeping I had awoken to a loud blast of opera at five a.m. I couldn't believe it. It had almost been a deal breaker.

She'd also waited until she thought I was asleep until she'd begin painting. Over time, she realised I was no threat, no encumbrance to her art, and so she'd painted whenever she felt like it and blasted her own ear drums with that racket she called music via the magic of iPod.

But I'd been aware of her restlessness last night. I'd had the strange feeling she'd wanted to talk. I was too tired to lift a finger, but now as Kimo called and began ranting to me about the missed day of work, I realised my energy was back.

"Take it easy, big guy," I said. "I'm ready for action."

It could go either way with Kimo when I tried to placate him, but this time it seemed to work.

"Okay. We got a guy who's been in an accident. Happened at three o'clock this morning, but his family didn't report it because he was drunk and they were afraid he'd get a ticket. Can you believe these people?"

"Unreal," I said. I couldn't actually believe these people. Bad accidents happened on our islands due to booze all the time. Especially single-vehicle collisions.

"He's being driven to the airport by the ambulance right now." Kimo sounded more worried now than pissed at me and that was a good thing.

"You're working with a new nurse today. Jon's still not up to par. Her name is Kate Stanmore. She'll pick you up. I know your car broke down yesterday. Be ready in ten minutes."

Shit! I leapt from the bed, raced to the bathroom and took a shower, letting the hot spray beat down on my skinny body. If I'd had any doubts about what had happened to me the day before, a mere glance in the steamy mirror made me wince. My body was covered in dings and scrapes. Malakai had fixed the worst of my injuries. Guess he thought I should take home some souvenirs. I'd have preferred a T-shirt.

I cleaned my teeth, ran some deodorant under my arms and rushed to the bedroom where I changed into working clothes, zipping up my jump suit. I could feel the adrenaline rush that always came with a new case.

The battle for life. The fear of death.

I understood Kimo's concern was a financial one. The patient's family might have been foolish in delaying getting the man help, but they could easily turn around and sue our company if the man died in our care or once he arrived in Honolulu.

Checking my gear, I heard a car horn outside then Evelin was by my side in the hallway.

"The last photo disappeared," she said. "Please tell me I didn't imagine it."

"You didn't imagine it." I stood and hugged her. She smelt of red wine and paint.

"Oh, sweetie, thank you!" She crumpled in my arms. "Thank you!" She was crying hot tears now, but I had no time for this. I would have comforted her any other time, but I had a medical emergency to attend. "These are the best paintings I've ever done," she said. "I would hate for it to have all come from my imagination."

"So what if it did?" I asked as the car horn honked again.

I unplugged my iPad and cell phone charger from the wall and picked up my kit. "The best art is borne of imagination," I reminded her.

In the living room, I was stunned to see how many paintings she'd done of the batterflies. It was quite eerie, really, like stumbling into the room and finding these beings here for real. They looked so lifelike.

"You have a case?" she asked, finally tuning into my panic.

"Yes."

The car horn honked again.

"Will you be back later?"

"Yes," I said as I ran out of the front door. She followed me as I reached Kate Stanmore's vehicle. She looked annoyed but relieved as we shook hands. I introduced her to Evelin.

I turned to my landlady then and thanked her for having my car towed the day before. "I owe you," I said.

"No, you don't. I'll tell you what's weird though. They couldn't find anything wrong with it." She shrugged. "Cars are like that."

I gave her a finger wave after stowing my kit in Kate's trunk and climbed into her passenger seat.

"Your girlfriend doesn't want you to go, huh?" Kate asked.

"She's not my girlfriend. She's my landlady. She's an artist. Been up painting all night."

"Ohhh," Kate said in a tone that I knew meant, *that explains it.*

"She seemed a little hyper." Kate waited for a response, but I had none. I didn't like talking about my friends.

We drove in virtual silence to the airport. I was busy establishing our patient's flight record from the information Kimo had texted to my iPad.

"How long have you been working with the company?" I asked when she'd glanced at me several times, clearly expecting me to make conversation.

"This is my second week."

Oh, boy, the floodgates opened.

"I've always wanted to live in Hawaii," she said. "I had no idea how expensive it is. I've had to take on three jobs just to make ends meet."

I glanced at her. "Sorry to hear that."

She took a hand off the steering wheel and gave a dismissive gesture.

"I'd been warned, but I ignored it. I thought people were being jealous and weird. I love it though and it's worth it."

She was beginning to thaw me out now. "How long have you been on island?" I asked her in the way we locals called it.

"Five months."

I nodded. I was back to business now, sending Kimo an email that we were pulling into the airfield.

My heart did a series of backflips when I saw that the plane was ready, the ambulance beside it and that our pilot was...

Alex.

He waved to us and I jumped out as Kate zoomed off to park.

"Hey, brah." He shook my hand as if he hadn't tried to drown me the day before. As if we were friends and everything was cool between us. What the fuck?

I was nervous as hell as Alex helped me wheel our passenger, Mr George Cannard, onto the aircraft. As soon as I looked at the grey-haired, caramel skinned Mr Cannard, I realised I knew the man but couldn't quite place him.

Thanking the paramedics who'd brought our patient here, I took the admission sheet from one of them. Nino. I remembered his name now. He waited for me to go over the sheet and he said, "I can't believe his family snuck him home and thought he'd be okay. I think it's a broken neck."

That explained all the packing on the old guy's head and neck, but paramedics frequently did this as a precaution.

Mr Cannard was already pleading for help. He was in agony.

"My neck hurts," he whined.

"What pain medication did you give him?" I asked Nino. I pointed to his sheet. "It says five ccs but I have no idea of what."

"Crap. Sorry. I gave him valium just to calm him down."

I closed my eyes. "Thanks."

"Guess the Fish House won't be getting its lobsters tonight," he said, which I thought was very insensitive.

I knew instantly who Mr Cannard was now. Yes, he was a lobster fisherman and rumoured to haul in the best crustaceans in the business, but he was also a former big wave surfer. He'd won competitions back in the sixties and still surfed for pleasure.

"See you, Nino," I said and climbed on board.

I hadn't realised Kate was waiting for me and I extended a hand to help her up into the plane. She'd obviously been listening to my conversation with Nino. She helped me secure our passenger and turn on the computer, searching for his file which I'd remotely uploaded to the system.

Alex gave me a thumbs-up from the cockpit and I began to focus on my patient.

As the senior nurse, I sat beside Mr Cannard and talked to him as Kate sat by his head, checking his vital stats now appearing on the computer monitor as I hooked him up with the computerised, digital pads.

I reassured the man, who, according to his medical records, was sixty-two. I called the hospital in Honolulu and the doctor on duty okayed me giving my patient eight hundred milligrams of Tylenol.

"It won't interfere with his Digoxin," he said.

"He's a heart patient?" That wasn't on his record. I typed it into my iPad as I kept talking to the doctor on my headset.

"Just diagnosed a week ago."

"He's been drinking," I said. "Reeks of it."

"Yeah, so his wife told me. He's been complaining of pain."

"Still is," I said, my tone clipped as the patient began whining again. I could never understand why people couldn't see what disastrous choices they made when drinking on top of taking a volatile medication like Digoxin.

He must have had a serious problem his physician wanted under control, but Digoxin, made from the foxglove plant, was one of those drugs dispensed under very strict supervision. Most doctors required their patients to come in for weekly appointments to check their lungs and blood pressure. The drug could cause vision problems and mental confusion in a sober person, let alone a guy who'd been drinking and was driving around in an unlit neighbourhood at three in the morning.

"I saw their eyes," he suddenly said to me.

"Excuse me?"

"The batterflies," he said. "I saw their eyes. They told me not to drive."

"Oh, boy, he's still stoned," Kate whispered as I ended the call to Honolulu.

But I knew he wasn't stoned. I had a feeling he'd been seeing batterflies and it threw me. Malakai had tried to protect the man so I knew he was a good person. He needed my help.

"How's his blood pressure?" I asked her, prepping a needle for him.

"Low."

"That's typical with Digoxin."

"Is it?" she seemed enthralled. "You are so poised. I'm freaking like hell over here."

"You're doing great," I assured her. "The low blood pressure means he's not going to start hyperventilating and suffering hypoxia." I hesitated, about to add, breathing problems, but she just nodded. Phew. She knew some things, then...

"Mr Cannard," I said, "I'm giving you a little something more for the pain." I injected him and Alex, whose job it was to listen, took this as his cue to start the taxi run. This was the most crucial part of any flight. Take-offs and landings in a patient with a possible broken neck or back could aggravate an injury.

"Cool," Mr Cannard said. "I feel cold."

Oh, that wasn't good. That was the low blood pressure.

"Kate, can you hand me the thermal blanket, please?"

She passed it to me and I was aware of her stare the entire time. As Alex picked up speed for take-off, my patient yelled, "My neck!"

"It's okay," I assured him, "I'm here. I won't let anything happen to you."

We took off, an exhilarating moment when one soars into the skies. I felt a pang of being separated from my beloved, but I felt safe in the knowledge nobody else would be claiming Malakai before I returned.

I tucked Mr Cannard in and he settled a little. "Doesn't hurt as much," he said.

"Good. I'm glad."

Kate was still watching everything I did. That was good. It would be the only way she'd learn. It was the way I had learned.

We had a good flight with Mr Cannard showing more courage than men half his age. The hospital's ambulatory unit waited for us on the tarmac and I thanked them as they took possession of our patient.

"God bless you," Mr Cannard said.

"And you, too, sir." He'd won me over with his determination not to whine more or give in to pain. I was so glad we'd got him here in a timely manner. Something made me go over and kiss his cheek.

"Be well, sir. Get better. I want to see you up and surfing very soon."

His eyes welled with tears. "Me, too," he said.

I hoped it wasn't just a…shared dream.

Turning to Kate, I saw the emotion in her face. "They told me you were the best, but you really are. You really care."

I smiled. "Yes, I do."

Kimo was in a good mood when we went inside.

"I know I got you both up early. You'll be flying back in a couple of hours. If you like, you can borrow my car and head to Zippy's on Nimitz Highway."

"Love me some Zippy's," Kate said.

"Expect a catch," I said. "What is it?"

Kimo acted shocked. "You're so untrusting, Jepoi." He cracked a grin. "Okay, okay, so I just want you to bring me a couple cherry napples."

"We can do that. Come on, Kate, let's wash our hands."

* * * *

Fifteen minutes later, we were sitting in the nice section of Zippy's, drinking coffee and eating eggs and toast. I was disappointed to feel full after a few bites of egg and half a slice of toast, because it all looked and tasted so great.

"You're not going to finish that?" Her predatory eyes gleamed.

I shook my head and slid her the plate. I could smell the cherry from Kimo's napples and had a sudden urge for red.

Blood. Oh, yeah. I wanted blood.

What the...?

I came back to reality and paid for the check.

"You're cute, you're a great nurse and generous on top of it?" Kate asked, licking butter from her fingertips. "I bet that means you're gay."

I burst into laughter. "Guilty as charged."

"It figures." Her face darkened for a moment.

We drove back to the airport and I tossed Kimo his car keys and greasy paper bag filled with napples. Kate and I slumped into seats against the wall, waiting for the flight home.

"Do you think Alex will be pissed that we didn't invite him to breakfast?" Kate asked.

"Alex doesn't eat breakfast."

"Oh. I didn't know that."

It was true, but the fact was that I hadn't even thought about it. He could have joined us for coffee and in the past he might have, but Kimo didn't like him leaving the plane. He'd have to prep it for the return flight home. I hadn't even *thought* about bringing him coffee. Kimo always had a pot in the office here, but in the recent past I would have brought Alex a cup and maybe even a napple just to be nice.

I realised I'd been especially tense on the flight because I'd had to trust him, that it was him. That he would bring us to Honolulu in safety.

That he wouldn't try to kill me mid-air.

Malakai had told me not to trust him. Not to be with him. Or Jon.

"Is he straight?" Kate asked, her tone low.

"Alex? Yes, I think so."

She looked a little happier now. As we waited, she filled me in on the story of her life. I was starting to feel a little sleepy, even with two cups of coffee inside me. It was always that way after an adrenaline rush.

Alex came to tell us we were ready to go and I was grateful Kate's sorry saga continued the whole flight home. I had a good excuse not to be able to give him any attention. I marvelled that she was able to talk without apparent pause for breath. And actually, Kate was a lot more interesting than most mainlanders I'd met. Actually, she was hilariously entertaining, especially when she got to the part about how she found the man of her dreams and he'd asked her to marry him.

After an exhaustive search, she'd found the perfect wedding dress but came home from her job as a teacher to find him dressed in her wedding dress and even her shoes, three days before their nuptials.

"I'd been walking around the house in my shoes for about a week before the wedding, you know, to get comfortable in them and I couldn't figure out why they suddenly felt so huge."

She'd called off the wedding, left him to return all their unopened gifts and had flown to the Big Island. She'd been a nurse at one point and after taking a crash course with our company and passing her certificate, she took on days whenever she could.

"I know if I can work full time with Hawaii Air Patrol I won't need to keep up my other two jobs," she said as we came in for a landing in Hilo. "You think that day might come?"

"Sure it will," I told her. "We all start part-time and I don't know how it happens, but eventually you find yourself with a busy schedule."

"I hope so," she said. As soon as we'd landed and had left the plane, she threw her arms around me. "You're so awesome, Jepoi! I hope we work together again, soon!"

She dropped me home, where I found Evelin painting more and more batterflies.

"I've emailed jpegs to a couple of stores in Honolulu and in Maui and Kona. I've had more orders for these than any other paintings I've done!" she told me and bent her head once more to her work.

I went to my room and fell on the bed, sleep catching up with me at last. I was too tired to get up and plug in my iPad and phone, but forced myself. It was a peculiar feeling of pain and exhaustion. I was so tired I crawled, yes crawled, to the wall and plugged them in. Back on my bed, fully clothed, I fell into a dreamy sleep where Malakai stripped me naked, his voice a beautiful echo, an echo of shells, oceans washing away in my mind.

His kisses claimed mine as he ran his hands over my body.

"Oh, yes," I said, aware I was talking. I felt his teeth scraping over my nipples, hardening my cock. I looked down my body as he began licking, sucking and enjoying my cock. I could see his red-black hair gleaming in the light streaming in between the slats of my green bamboo blinds.

His teeth. Oh, his teeth. In spite of his vampire state, he worked tenderly on my cock, sucking me in with care. I cried out with the pleasure-pain of his bite against my shaft. He sucked me with total ownership, his canines receding as he took me all the way into his mouth. I felt his tongue lying warm and flat against my cockhead as he drew his mouth up, felt his fingertips at my hole.

He coaxed pure joy from me, one finger then two working their way into me. I opened my legs, desire and filmy, foamy dreams lapping at the edges of my mind as I came in his mouth, his fingers working their strange, yet familiar magic on me.

My cell phone rang and I bolted awake.

No Malakai, but I was naked, and I'd come. All over myself.

I took the call. Another emergency. Of course.

Hurrying to throw on clothes and get out of the house, I had just arrived out front when Kate pulled up to collect me.

"We meet again," she said, wiggling her eyebrows.

As she drove, I worked on my iPad. A man had been found unconscious in the middle of the street just off the volcano road. No ID. Nothing.

He was alive but unresponsive.

Paramedics were unloading him as we arrived on the tarmac.

I almost fell over when I saw him.

It was Malakai.

Chapter Eight

Felix kept talking in my head. *"Why in hell didn't you stay in that old man's body, Kane? You're so...recognisable."*

"Don't you think Del knows who I am?"

Felix agreed. *"And I will not subject another human to injury. I was sure he'd make his move on the way here. Instead he taunted me the entire way about how I was aging badly and blah, blah, blah. Will Mr Cannard survive?"*

"Of course he'll survive. He has a sore neck that's all. I fixed his other problems as compensation for scaring him to death. He'll make a miraculous recovery in hospital and come out healthier than he's even been. Hell, he'll be able to surf again."

"Nice move, Kane. Now, what are you going to do?"

"Hopefully I can send Jepoi a message to act casually. Although I have played unresponsive, I know he hasn't stopped staring at me. What I can't believe is that Veil would lower himself to take on the persona of a poor, young nurse. And Jepoi appears to have been taken in by her hook, line and...sinker."

"Be careful, Kane. I told you this was a very bad idea. Starzs agrees. He says that –"

"Okay. Enough, Felix! Shut up now. You are truly giving me a headache."

I heaved an inward sigh as silence filled my brain. The young woman was looking down at me. No one noticed those eyes burning, but I could feel them trying to penetrate my soul. *"Kane, you have the balls of a...I don't know what!"*

"I could say the same for you, Deacon Veil. What's a low-life underworld demon like you doing hanging out with Kanaloa's main squeeze?"

"He used to be yours, didn't he? Word is, he wants you back."

"Don't act like he can't hear you. I know he's here, in Alex."

"Um," Veil said. *"How do you like my hair, Kane? Think you could get hot for me? Or is it only the sweet little succulent mortal who tempts you? Poor soul. He's halfway to becoming a blood sucker like you. You want to spread that curse around, do you?"*

"I've tried to protect him by giving him some of my blood. There are obvious...side effects. They'll wear off."

"He's fawning over you. And oh my, what a good little nurse I make. Shall I cut off your balls? A girl does have the right to make some mistakes when she's in training."

"I will kick your ass back to the place you belong, Deacon. Won't be long!"

There was silence then. He was Kate, doing Kate things with Jepoi, who frantically was checking me all over for some signs of injury. I'd imitated all the human signs, including pulse and heartbeat, but I couldn't do it for long. What I could do was bring down this plane somewhere and force these charlatans to reveal themselves so I could save Jepoi. I knew they couldn't wait to get their hands on him, to kill him. I would never let that happen.

"Kane. I love you."

Fever

That was Delmontre. I intended to ignore him.

Jepoi was speaking in my ear. "Malakai. Malakai, please. It's me. Open your eyes."

"You know him?" The nurse spoke, feigning innocence. "He's really hot. Did you fuck him?"

"Jepoi, don't answer her. Be careful."

"Kate?" Jepoi paused. "Did you just tell me to be careful?"

"No." A female laugh pierced my ears. "I asked if you'd fucked him. He is so beautiful. I bet many have wanted to fuck him."

"Deacon. Enough!"

"I'm having a bit of fun, that's all!"

"Is he good?" the female voice asked.

"I...I don't know him," Jepoi replied.

I made sure Deacon heard me laughing. *A man of discretion.*

"I can get him to say what I want. I can slice into his memory bank and watch you fuck him."

"Not before I cut you in half."

The female voice went silent.

"Where are we going?" Jepoi suddenly asked. "Alex, this isn't the way to—"

That was my cue. I opened my eyes, sat straight up and grabbed Jepoi by the wrist. He gasped, his eyes widening. "Malakai? What...?"

The plane started to descend as I pointed down. The nurse and Alex pressed together. They laced their powers together to force the plane up again and as we strained, the plane pushed up and down, back and forth like a boat on a rocking sea.

"Malakai!" Jepoi clung to me. "What's happening?"

I glanced at him. I knew he saw something in my eyes he hadn't seen before. He gasped and sank to the floor. "Stay there. Don't move!"

175

My voice filled the plane, rattling the windows and seats. Alex and Kate slowly bent down and went to their knees in front of me. I held them there with all the power I had left as a fierce wind blew and the plane went tunnelling to the ground.

We landed on a deserted stretch of beach, one I'd thrown a barrier around. They weren't going anywhere. I watched casually as my two nemeses scrambled to their feet and pushed through the emergency exit. I turned to extend my hand to Jepoi, who sat frozen to the spot. "Are you all right?" I asked.

He nodded wordlessly.

"Stay here." I slowly made my way outside. I stood on the beach, my feet sinking into the warm sand, and surveyed the bodies of Kate and Alex running in circles, trying to find a way out. I glanced up at the silvery moon then began to walk towards them.

They began to bellow then grovel. They felt my rage and they knew what that rage could do.

Veil flung himself at my feet, but I kicked him away and he went hurling across the sand. Delmontre was next. "Let me explain, my love."

"You insult me with your endearment," I said. "I have warned you to stay away from the mortal. How many times have I done so, Delmontre?"

"You cannot hurt me. I am his, under his protection." He came closer.

I looked into eyes that were not his. "You have no right to this body or this soul. Give them back."

"Or what?" he threw at me. "What will you do to me that you haven't already done? You've torn out my heart, forgotten your love for me, exchanged it for sex with this filthy, useless mortal!"

He pointed and I turned to see Jepoi standing on the sand a few feet behind me. He now knew much more than I'd ever intended. "Jepoi, get back!"

Delmontre began to take a step towards Jepoi and I lifted my arm. Alex's body flew in the air and slid across the sand almost to the waters' edge.

Jepoi was tugging at my arm. "No, Malakai. Don't hurt Alex."

"It's not Alex," I said. "Now, do as I tell you and..."

The nurse came closer, a tongue darting around her lips, a huge fork at the tip. "I want his soul," she screamed.

"Kate!" Jepoi said. He looked at me with such questions, questions I had no time to answer.

Delmontre was approaching again. The earth began to tremble and lightning crackled in the sky. "You see, I told you Kanaloa would never let you hurt me! I am his."

"Kanaloa?" Jepoi muttered beside me. "Malakai. I..."

"He is not Malakai, you fool!" Delmontre gave Jepoi a rakish smile. "This is —"

"Delmontre, no!" I told him. I reached out and took him by the throat and again the lightning crackled in the sky. I glanced up and released him.

He fell to his knees laughing, his hands reaching out to my thighs as he tried to lean his head against my groin. I pushed him away.

"What does Alex mean?" Jepoi insisted. "Not Alex...but who is he?"

"Who am I?" Delmontre got to his feet. "I am his lover. I am the one he loves. I made a mistake. I gave him up, but I was wrong. And he is mine, Jepoi. Not yours. Never yours."

"You have another...lover?" Jepoi searched my face. Such pain in his eyes.

"No," I sighed. "You don't understand, Jepoi. It was long ago and..."

"Malakai, I don't—"

"Tell him! Tell him, Malakai," the nurse sneered. "Tell him who you really are!"

"Go back to hell where you came from!" I let out a roar and the earth opened in front of me. With one swipe of my hand, I sent Veil hurtling down under. Then I closed the gap.

"You realise the nurse's soul is forfeit," Delmontre sniggered. "That's one for me."

Jepoi was shaking his head. "You killed...Kate!"

"Listen, it wasn't Kate. It was..."

"Yes, Malakai," Delmontre mocked. "Tell him who Kate was."

I grabbed Jepoi and began to walk back to the plane.

"You going to leave Alex out here to die?" Delmontre yelled after us.

Jepoi was fighting me. "We can't leave him here to die, Malakai. Please." His eyes were filled with tears.

Damn it. "You don't know what you're asking," I said.

"I don't understand any of it," Jepoi groaned. "Kate is gone, sucked into the ground and...Alex..."

"Isn't Alex," I told him.

"He was your lover."

"No, not...yes...but..."

Jepoi turned his back on me. I sighed then stuck out my head and motioned to Delmontre. "Come on."

Delmontre stepped on board. "Lover's quarrel?" He gave me a satisfied grin. "*Now I won't have to kill him. At least not today. Do I get a reward for that, lover? How about a fuck?*"

Fever

I showed him my finger. "Fuck this."

He laughed. "Nice. You've become so very...common."

I got behind the controls and started the plane. Jepoi sat silently in his seat. Delmontre in Alex's body sat beside me.

We were up in the air within minutes and that's when it started to rain so heavily that I couldn't see a thing. I glared at Delmontre. "Your doings?"

"You know I don't have that power. I think it might be Kanaloa. He wants to see you."

"Well, I don't want to see him."

"You realise that if anyone has put that utterly confused mortal back there in danger, it has been you."

I didn't reply.

"Things could be so easy. You and I could challenge him. The council is yours, Kane, you know that. They love you. Kanaloa has become stale. He knows nothing of the world—is out of step. You are...well"— he squeezed my thigh—"beautiful!"

I'd had enough now. I reached over and opened the passenger door.

"Malakai, what are you doing?" Jepoi shouted frantically.

I undid Delmontre's seatbelt.

"So you want to fool around?" He grinned.

"Malakai, no!" Jepoi tried to grab my arm.

I yanked away and met Delmontre's gaze. "Give the body a soft landing somewhere or I'll make you pay! Now"—I gave him a shove—"get the fuck out of this plane!"

Jepoi let out a cry as the body dropped out and I closed the door. "What did you do? You killed them both. I don't understand you. I..."

The plane was rocking through the rain, a rain that was turning to hail. "Jepoi, sit down and put on the seat belt."

The hail began to pelt the plane, sounding like a thousand fists slamming into it.

Jepoi took the seat Delmontre had vacated. I could tell he was very upset. I reached over and took his hand. He pulled away. "Let me explain."

"Explain what? I…" His voice faltered.

"Wait!" I needed to get us out of this. There was nothing Kanaloa could do to me, but he could kill Jepoi. I closed my eyes. "Enough!"

The skies cleared, the hail stopped and I lowered the plane, imagining my safe house. *"Coming home, Felix."*

"Good, cause all hell has broken loose, my friend."

"Wonderful!"

When Jepoi saw the house in the distance, I thought he'd be happy. Instead, he said, "I want to go home."

"You can't, just yet," I said softly. "But I promise you, I'll make it so. I'll make it so you can go home safely again."

"How?" He turned to me as I landed the plane. "By you leaving me?"

I sighed.

He grabbed my hand. "I don't understand who or what you are. I can't even believe in my own senses anymore. My common sense tells me you murdered two people back there. Yet, everything inside me tells me you're not a murderer. Are you? Are you a murderer?"

"No," I said.

"How did you open the earth? How did you make the hail stop? Who was that inside of Alex claiming to be your lover?"

"Delmontre."

"Then he was your lover?"

I nodded.

"How did he get inside of Alex?"

"He made some shady deals, a bargain with Deacon Veil." I saw his confusion. "It's a long story, Jepoi, and the less you know…"

"I think you can tell me now," he said. "You need to. Let me ask you something, did you send vampire butterflies to watch over me and Evelin?"

I nodded.

"You are not of this world."

"On the contrary," I said. "I am this world."

"Then your name is not Malakai, as Alex said. He wanted to say your name. What is it?"

"I can't," I said. "It is forbidden. Let's go inside. Felix is waiting." I took his arm and we walked together into the house. "Don't worry," I added, "Alex will be all right."

"And Kate?"

I sighed. "I cannot say." I doubted very much if Deacon would spare her. He would take her soul in payment, and throw her body on a heap to rot. But I preferred not to give Jepoi too much detail.

Felix leapt into my arms when he saw me. "I was so worried." He glanced at Jepoi. "Guest again?"

"Make up the guest room," I said. He hopped off me and nodded. "We need to talk."

"About?" I asked.

"Starzs."

"Where is he?"

"You won't like it." He winced.

"Spill it!"

"He was lured away. I just got a communication from him. Want to know what he said?"

"Yes."

"He says Del has him and is forcing him to conjure sex dreams for you and he to meet."

I sighed. "That swine."

"Sex dreams?" Jepoi interjected.

"Yes, and I wouldn't sleep tonight, Jepoi," Felix cautioned.

"Why?" Jepoi and I demanded in unison.

"He plans to make Jepoi an observer in the dreams, wants Jepoi to know how it once was between you." Felix turned to Jepoi and fanned himself. "And oh my, when a god and…"

"Felix!" I intercepted quickly. "Silence. Go and cook!"

"I thought you wanted me to make up the bed."

"No need. Jepoi will stay in my room tonight." I turned to him. "We won't sleep."

Jepoi actually blushed. "What will we be doing then?"

"Talking," I said.

"Talking?" He made a face.

"Jepoi. If you sleep, you'll…"

"See you and your lover fucking your brains out?" His voice turned cold. "If you want him, then…"

I grabbed his shoulders. "I don't want him."

"He's certainly gone to a lot of trouble to have you." Jepoi sighed heavily. "What is he exactly?"

"He's a little twit."

"No, Malakai." Jepoi took my hand. "What-is-he?"

"A nobody, piggybacking on powers he doesn't fully understand. Now, enough about him."

"Am I ever going to know what I'm into here? You're some kind of vampire god, or…what are you fighting, other vampires?"

I sighed. "I'm not a…" I paused, tempered what I was about to say. "Being a god has nothing to do with the vampire in me. Like I said, it's complicated. Things have gone completely out of whack. You shouldn't be involved at all."

"But I am involved," he said, moving closer. "I…I love you, Malakai. Maybe I shouldn't. I've seen you do things that… God"—he moved away—"sometimes it's like a dream."

"Don't say dream," I told him. "It has quite a different connotation. Listen, Jepoi, some will do all they can to keep you from me. You need to resist your attraction to me. I've not helped that I know because…well…I'm drawn to you too."

"No," Jepoi said. "You're not drawn to me. You love me." He met my gaze.

I was surprised at his boldness, but he was right. I did. I couldn't acknowledge that. I turned away just as Felix yelled out that supper was ready.

I knew Felix didn't approve of Jepoi being here. He saw Jepoi as the source of the problem, but he wasn't. He was just the excuse. We went into the kitchen and Felix put down a hearty bowl of macaroni and cheese. I gave him a look.

"What?" He jumped onto the table and watched Jepoi as he sat down. "Try it."

With what few guests we have here, Felix serves macaroni and cheese?

However Jepoi seemed to enjoy it. He scoffed it down and asked for more. "So strange," he said. "I haven't had much of an appetite lately, but this is so good. I could eat and eat it."

I glanced at Felix suspiciously and when Jepoi was busy eating I crooked my finger at him. He followed me reluctantly. "What did you put in it?"

"Macaroni…cheese…"

A.J. Llewellyn and D.J. Manly

"Felix! Why is Jepoi stuffing his face with that stuff?"

"I added some of your blood supply and a little bit of sleeping potion." He backed up when he saw my face. "It's for your own good, master!"

"Don't call me...how could you?"

"I...I figured if...he could see more...was stronger and...if he saw the dreams of you and Del...he'd go away for good and we...well...we could have our life back." Tears ran down his face.

I groaned then rushed into the kitchen. "Jepoi, stop eating the..." I trailed off as I saw Jepoi, fast asleep, with his face in the macaroni and cheese. I turned and glared at Felix. "If I find that you are conspiring with Delmontre in any way..." I threatened.

"I wouldn't, Kane, I wouldn't." He shook his head, chewing on his thumbnail.

"I warned you not to talk to Delmontre, listen to his sob stories!" I picked Jepoi up in my arms. "Wipe his face!" I told Felix.

Quickly he got a wet cloth and wiped Jepoi's face off. I pushed him away and carried Jepoi to my bed. Felix followed, fretting all the way. "He was sad, but I wouldn't side with him. He was my friend and you two were...beautiful...together."

I lay Jepoi down and scowled at Felix.

"At one time," he qualified, "but not now."

"Get out," I told him. "Close the door."

He scurried away. I heard the door close behind him. I sat on the side of the bed and stroked Jepoi's face. He was out cold which meant he'd dream the dream of Delmontre and I together. I had to sleep too, I had to go into the dream with him, explain what he was seeing. It was so long ago. *Damn you, Delmontre!* Would he tell all? Would Jepoi know what I was, who

I was, when the dream was over? What were the consequences of that? It meant Jepoi could never go back to a normal life. He'd be with me...forever. Would that be so bad? Yes, he was a mortal being. I was not. How in the hell would we make this work?

It was forbidden to begin with and I already had enough marks against me. Heaven only knew what the punishment was for that.

I lay down beside Jepoi and closed my eyes, waiting for the worst to come. It wouldn't matter if I couldn't make him see I no longer loved Delmontre, that he'd betrayed me, left me hating him for what he'd done...no, the dream wouldn't show that at all.

When it began, Jepoi was walking down a dimly lit corridor and I followed. Starzs was leading him from one world to another. Suddenly we were bathed in light. I reached out to Jepoi to try to communicate with him, but something was preventing me. Like some sort of echoing wall, I was locked behind it.

I knew Delmontre would pull out all the stops. The setting was a cloud-like place where we'd had sex many times. The sex I'd had with Delmontre had gone the limits, straddling the line of pain and pleasure. Delmontre worshipped my status as a god, and loved to play homage to it. He craved my body like a drug and I, as drug dealer, fulfilled his every need. It was surreal, the room filled with sound and smell. I could almost taste the sex as Delmontre slid down my naked, wet body then looked directly at Jepoi.

Jepoi seemed at once sexually aroused yet enraged. I heard him whisper several times, "He's mine."

I placed my hand on the wall barrier between us and whispered back, "Yes, I am."

"Malakai." Jepoi reached out.

Delmontre fell back, my cock in his hand and again he looked at Jepoi. "Not Malakai. Look at him, his body, this cock...are you that daft, Jepoi...to not see? He is not Malakai...he is a deity. He is Kane. One of the major ruling gods of all the Hawaiian Islands."

I closed my eyes in despair.

Jepoi's mouth opened. He didn't say anything, but he stared at my image on that bed, an image that now slowly fucked his lover, rocking him on air. Delmontre let his head go back. He moaned out his need, his pleasure. "Mine!"

"How?" Jepoi went to his knees.

"A very naughty god." Delmontre grunted, pushing upward so that my image fucked him deeper and harder. "He was cursed by Kanaloa, sent to walk the earth as a vampire. A naughty, naughty, boy, right, Kane?" Delmontre reached up and scraped his nails down my chest. I opened my mouth and revealed sharp, vampire fangs.

"This was us," Delmontre cried out, coming now all over me. "This was us, and will be again. And you can't have him. You don't belong, Jepoi. So...go away and leave him be. Or I'll make sure you—"

"No!" Jepoi cried out suddenly, standing up.

I saw Jepoi march forward. He grabbed Delmontre and pulled him away from my image. Both images faded and I discovered that Jepoi had straddled my hips. He had my shirt open and was slowly circling my nipples with his tongue. He reached down and frantically began to undo my pants and before I could utter a word, he pinned my hands above my head, holding them to the mattress.

He stared into my eyes. "You're mine, Kane. So fuck me. Take me the way you took him in that dream, deep and hard and slow at first then...don't hold back anything. I want you. I want you now!"

I didn't argue. I wanted him as much as he did me. The dream had not had the effect Delmontre intended. In fact, it had made Jepoi horny as hell, and right now, that suited me fine. I began stripping him of his clothes, throwing them aside. I kissed his neck, his chest, took his cock into my mouth and ravished it with my lips and my tongue. Then I pushed Jepoi roughly to his knees on the bed and pressed his head forward. I took my time rimming him completely until he was gasping, pleading. I sank my cock into him, impaling him with it, deep and slow like he'd asked. I lifted him with one hand off the ground and tormented his cock and his nipples as I went deeper with my cock, making sure he didn't come until I'd finished pumping him hard and fast.

At one point, I pulled out and turned him around to face me. His legs on my shoulders, I went into him again without mercy, to the hilt, and he cried out. This time, it was my name. "Kane! Kane!"

I fucked him some more on the bed, moving from side to side, slow then fast, going in and out of him until he sobbed with relief. Then I lay down beside him and pulled him close into my arms.

He met my gaze. Softly, he said my name, "Kane."

I smiled at him.

"I saw the beginning, heaven and earth...creation...as you were fucking me. It was incredible. Did you do that for me?"

I nodded. "Yes."

He took my cock in his hand and stroked it then hunkered down and captured it with his mouth. He sat back and studied my erection then he straddled my hips, moving my cock between his ass cheeks, smiling at me.

I grunted. "Tease," I accused, cuffing his erection.

He grabbed my cock in hand and slid it up to his opening. Holding my gaze, he bore down. I clenched my teeth and let my head go back, moving my hips only at his invitation as he used my cock for his pleasure.

He came all over my stomach then sucked me to release a few minutes later. When he lay on my chest, still caressing my cock.

I glanced at him. I'd never met a hornier mortal than Jepoi. "Are you happy?"

He stroked my face. "Yes. Please don't send me away. I love you."

"I know," I said. "And now that you know who I am, I can never send you away. Oh, Jepoi, I'm so sorry. I've taken your life like Veil takes souls. I will be punished."

"Punished by whom?"

"The council."

"There's a council?"

"Yes."

"How does a god become a...?" He trailed off. "Is it true what Delmontre told me in the dream, that you were bad?"

"Kanaloa and I are supposed to rule together. We had a fight."

"About?"

"Our relationship."

"You were Kanaloa's lover too?" He sat up.

I pulled him back down with a smile. "It's difficult to explain. Anyway, he got angry, hooked up with a sorcerer and an ancient vampire and I was cursed to roam the earth as this."

"And Delmontre?"

"He is Kanaloa's slut now."

"Doesn't seem that way. He wants you back."

"He is fickle." I shrugged.

Jepoi actually laughed. "I feel as if I'm in some sort of movie. I can't believe it yet I've seen things…"

"That's why mortals are usually not involved." I hugged him closer. "I will protect you, Jepoi."

"Do you still love him?"

"Who? Kanaloa or Del?"

"Either," Jepoi sounded irritated.

I laughed. "You are jealous."

"Stop it." He hit me. "What do you want?"

"Besides you?"

He smiled. "Yes. Besides me?" He kissed me tenderly on the mouth.

"Peace," I said, "just peace." I didn't want to go into all that now. One day, I would need to get rid of this curse and face Kanaloa. I would have to restore the balance to a world that was filled with pain and strife. I wasn't sure where Jepoi would fit in all that. I just knew that right now I wanted Jepoi beside me here in this bed.

Jepoi was falling asleep. "Good night," he said softly. "Oh, yes and" — he held his middle finger up in the air — "good night, Del!"

My eyes widened a little, but I found myself smiling as I snuggled closer to him and heard his breathing grow shallow in sleep. I was sure Del must have appreciated that finger.

I was almost asleep when I felt the house move under me. Felix was on the bed shouting. I sat up. Jepoi did too, crying out, "What's happening? What's happening?"

Felix was talking so fast I couldn't make sense of it. I finally grabbed him to me and forced him to slow down. "Take a breath. Now, tell me. What in the world is happening?"

"It's...it's Kanaloa..." Felix gulped. "He's here and he wants a meeting."

About the Authors

A.J. Llewellyn

A.J. Llewellyn lives in California, but dreams of living in Hawaii. Frequent trips to all the islands, bags of Kona coffee in the fridge and a healthy collection of Hawaiian records keep this writer refueled.

A.J. never lacks inspiration for male/male erotic romances and on the rare occasions this happens, pursues other passions such as collecting books on Hawaiiana, surfing and spending time with friends and animal companions.

A.J. Llewellyn believes that love is a song best sung out loud.

D.J. Manly

I write not only for my own pleasure, but for the pleasure of my readers. I can't remember a time in my life when I haven't written and told stories. When I'm not writing, I'm dreaming about writing. Eroticism between consenting adults, in all its many forms is the icing on the cake of life but one does not live by sex alone. The story of how two people find love in spite of the odds is what really turns me on.

You can find their contact information, website details and author profile pages at http://www.totallybound.com.

Totally Bound Publishing